The Paris Deception

Neither Despise Nor Fear Book 2

V M Knox

V M Knox

ISBN: 978-0-6457048-6-0

Any references to historical events, real people, or real places are used fictitiously. Names, characters, and places are products of the author's imagination.

Front cover image by Brittany Wilson.

First printing edition 2025.

www.vmknoxauthor.com

The Paris Deception

Neither Despise Nor Fear Book 2

V M Knox

V M Knox

AUTHOR'S NOTE

Although this story is entirely fictitious, the character of Alistair Quinn is based on a real man.

BUT

WARNING!!!

Spoiler Alert! You really should read Book One in this series entitled

Neither Despise Nor Fear

Before you read *The Paris Deception*

You've been warned!

For

Peter

23.06.54 – 13.08.24

Preface

London

14th August 1966

'You don't have to do this.'

'I know. But when will we get another such opportunity?'

'Even with all your training and expertise, there is no guarantee that this will work. Or that you'll ever be seen again.'

'Promise me that Vlatkov will remain in prison and I'll be safe enough.'

She nodded. 'They've done wonders with your appearance. And the doctors have done a great job breaking your nose.'

'Even his own mother, if he has one, won't be able to tell us apart.'

'Fortunately she won't ever see you side by side.' She paused and straightened the collar of his coat. 'Only break cover for something really important.'

'I'm not stupid, Grace.'

'You have the bag?'

'Of course.' He smiled. 'If I didn't know better, I'd say you were worried about me.'

'Not worried. Concerned. We can't have any mishaps. Too many lives at stake.'

'Especially mine.' He left her then.

A car was outside waiting to take him to the airport. From now on he was Vasali Vlatkov, former Soviet KGB agent captured in Finland and now being traded for a British citizen arrested in Moscow for espionage.

CHAPTER ONE

East Berlin
Wednesday 17th July 1968

Grigori Ivkin was not a young man. What he lacked in youthful stamina, he made up for in knowledge gained from years of practicing his craft. At fifty-five, he was a master spy. Deception was his stock in trade. And lies had kept him alive.

Just before midnight, he left his apartment on the top floor of a grey stone building on the Majakowski Ring and hurried down the unembellished dark stairwell to the ground floor. He opened the door to the street and stepped outside. Despite being summer, it was a cool night. Above him, the moon cast its insouciance over the street, its beams lending a monochrome hue to the night. For one second he stared at the night sky; distant, remote, detached. Familiar. Glancing in both directions, he crossed the road and walked towards the park at the end of his street, avoiding the dim yellow glow of the overhead streetlights. He pulled his coat around him, the gesture more from habit than cold then lit a cigarette. Nothing stirred but a few stray cats scurrying between the shadows. But then, the Majakowski Ring was an area reserved for senior members of the Stasi and, like himself, trusted officers of the KGB. No junior officer or passing stranger would dare to question the late-night activities of those who resided here.

As he entered the park, he flicked his cigarette butt into the bushes and then reached into his pocket for his cigarette case, the action automatic. Taking another out, he lit it. From habit, his eyes scanned the park for moving shadows, but he sensed he was alone. His mind turned to the man he'd been watching for two years. The KGB had arranged the accidental meeting at a scientific conference where Kurt Friedleman, a senior East German scientist had presented a paper on radar, a subject in which Ivkin had feigned interest. Friedleman worked at the top-secret scientific facility coughing distance from Stasi Headquarters in Normannenstrasse. In the two years Ivkin had been studying the man, he'd learned a great deal about Friedleman's habits. He knew who Friedleman met, who he spent time with, who he slept with, what his interests were, what he ate, and how much he drank. And, he knew the man's fascination with art, and sculpture in particular. Ivkin drew back on his cigarette, the strong Russian tobacco filling his lungs. Over time, the friendship had yielded more information than just the man's idiosyncrasies; Ivkin knew how the scientist thought. The man was an academic, but like many of his breed, he was also an introvert. Single-minded about his work but also nervous. Afraid. Malleable. All the human traits that were exploitable. Moreover, Ivkin believed Friedleman's vulnerability made him a risk. Then, three weeks ago, over a late-night vodka drinking session in Friedleman's flat, Ivkin had struck espionage gold. He'd learned of a seemingly inconsequential personal habit; Friedleman kept a notebook on his bedside table in case a thought came to him in the night.

Ivkin knew from experience that it was always the little things that made a man exploitable. Personal habits, instinctive and routine that condemned a naïve man so completely. Ivkin dropped the cigarette butt on the pavement and stamped it out. He checked his watch and then lit another *Laika* cigarette. Once through the park, he turned into the street where Friedleman and his wife, Marlis lived. Ivkin halted just outside the rim of light cast by the streetlight and inhaled deeply, his gaze on the apartment building opposite. It was much like his own, only plainer. Kurt and Marlis Friedleman lived on the second floor. Ivkin checked his watch. Midnight. From previous surveillance, he knew the bedroom light would be switched off soon. With his gaze on the second-floor window, he flicked the *Laika* butt into the gutter then felt for the lock picks in his coat pocket.

The light went off.

He waited thirty minutes. A light breeze rustled the nearby trees and lifted a discarded sheet of newspaper into the night. Somewhere in the distance, he heard a car, but no one drove down this street. He stepped from the curb and crossed the road, his eyes flicking left and right. Standing in the darkened portico, he checked the street again then withdrew the lock-pick in his pocket and inserted it into the main entry door. It slid easily back. He slipped inside, closing the door quietly, then climbed the stairs, making less noise than a panther. He knew the flat. He'd been there many times with his wife, Ludmilla. The two couples spent time together; happy evenings in each other's homes, playing cards and drinking cheap Russian vodka late into the night. But for Ivkin it had always been about surveillance. Friedleman had no idea of his real status or position with the KGB. Or that their initial meeting had been anything other than accidental. In fact,

Friedleman believed Ivkin held a low-ranking position as a records clerk with the Stasi; a misconception Ivkin had been careful to cultivate. Along with his real purpose; the cultivation of trust. That vital ingredient needed to accomplish complete control.

Grigori gripped the door handle as the locks turned in the barrel. He paused, then stepped inside and waited for his eyes to become accustomed to the darkened room. In the quiet stillness, he could hear snoring. He closed the door to the stairwell and crept along the hall.

Stepping inside the bedroom, he saw Kurt and Marlis sleeping. Ivkin edged towards the left side of the bed. He stared at Kurt, the mouth open, his yellow-stained teeth, the eyes moving violently, and half closed in REM sleep. Ivkin's gaze coursed quickly around the room. On the bedside table sat the small black notebook and pencil. Reaching for it, he opened it and flipped through the pages. It was filled with sketches. Some were crossed out, others worked over multiple times. He closed it and slipped it along with the pencil into his pocket. Retracing his steps, he tiptoed through the apartment, relocking the door as he left.

Once home, he went straight to the bedroom to check on Ludmilla. She still lay on her left side, and he surmised she had not woken. He walked into the bathroom and changed back into his pajamas, hanging his clothes on the coat hanger on the back of the door. But sleep would be impossible for at least several hours. He went to the sitting room and poured himself a vodka. Downing it in one gulp, he poured another and then lit a cigarette. Satisfied his wife had not woken, he slumped into a chair then opened the notebook and scrutinised the drawings. Given Friedleman's area of scientific expertise, Ivkin believed he was staring at an antenna, but the dimensions were staggering. It resembled the scaffolding around a non-existent multi-storey building. He drew on his cigarette and considered the ramifications of such a device as the clock in the kitchen rhythmically ticked away time. With such an antenna, the USSR would be capable of picking up signals miles away, perhaps even thousands of miles away. Ivkin closed the notebook and stared into the air before him. He considered the possibility that Friedleman's invention could have over-the-horizon capabilities. Despite recent developments in the fledgling space industry, he knew this invention could change the balance of power in an already jittery world. Holding the notebook, he stood, placed it into his coat which hung on the hook behind the front door, then returned to bed, his mind alive at what he'd just seen.

***

Thursday 18th July 1968

At six, Ivkin woke and went to the bathroom. He could hear Ludmilla wake and get out of bed. He knew the well-rehearsed routine; she would reach for her dressing gown and then make their bed, unless it was washing day when sheets and pillowcases would be scattered about the floor. 'An early start, Grigori?' he heard her shout.

He reached for his razor before responding. 'Yes. I have meetings all day.'

'You work too hard. I'll cook you a good breakfast, so you won't be hungry.' He heard her shuffle along the hall towards the kitchen. A *good* breakfast, he knew from experience was two eggs, fried toast, mushrooms and coffee. He had between ten and fifteen minutes to shave, wash and dress before his breakfast was cooked.

Stepping from the shower, he wrapped a towel around him and checked the hall. He could hear the noises in the kitchen. Hurrying, he dressed then placed his briefcase on the bed and packed an extra jumper, a wash bag and a spare pair of glasses. Pausing only for a second, he moved the bed aside, exposing a small cavity he'd made in the wall behind the bedhead. It held his miniature camera, some American dollars and several passports. Concealing the camera, money and passports in the lining of his hat, he carried it and his light overcoat to the sitting room then went to the kitchen to eat.

A plate of eggs, mushrooms and fried bread sat waiting for him, a mug of steaming coffee sat beside it. Ivkin sat down. 'Looks delicious! As always.'

Ludmilla beamed, her eyes bright and her smile wide. 'Will you be home late?'

'I think that is possible,' he said, devouring the meal.

Drinking the last of the hot coffee, he stood and walked into the lounge room to collect his coat and satchel. Ludmilla came from the kitchen and kissed his cheek. 'Take care, Grigori. Have a good day!'

'You too.'

Ivkin closed the front door and ran down the stairs. With no need for stealth, his footsteps echoed in the concrete stairwell. Outside, a car was parked by the curb. As he strode towards it, the driver got out. Ivkin nodded to the unknown heavy-set man some twenty or more years younger than himself. There would be no introduction and no conversation.

It was a short journey. The car pulled up outside Friedleman's apartment building. Ivkin went to the door and rang the bell for Kurt's apartment. A minute later, he heard Marlis's voice.

'Good morning, Grigori. He's running a little late this morning. Would you like to come up?'

'Thank you. I will.'

The door was open when he knocked at the door to flat 4.

'Come in, Grigori. He's nearly ready,' Marlis called from the kitchen.

He stepped inside and stood in the sitting room that could have been his own.

Marlis came from the kitchen to greet him. 'I can't tell you how hard it's been not telling anyone about where Kurt is going. It's all so exciting! Thank you so much for going with him this morning. He's in quite a state,' she added. 'He's not his usual self, although I think it's probably just nerves. You don't go to the West every day. Especially Paris.'

Ivkin nodded. 'He'll be fine. But may I remind you, Marlis, no talk. Not even with your neighbours. No one is to know where Kurt is going.'

'Of course. I understand.'

'I hope so. No discussion with anyone, Marlis, and that includes Ludmilla.'

'You haven't told her Kurt is going to Paris?'

'No! And you are not to tell her either.'

Marlis nodded. 'But you cleared it with the authorities, didn't you?'

'Naturally! He couldn't go otherwise. But there is no point in drawing unnecessary attention. We don't want anyone thinking there is more to his visit to Paris other than to meet with the Head Curator at the Louvre Museum.'

'Morning, Grigori,' Kurt said appearing in the sitting room.

Ivkin watched the scientist fuss with his belongings. 'You seem anxious, Kurt. Do you have everything you need? All the papers and the invitation from the Head Curator?'

Friedleman pulled on his coat and leaned towards his wife, kissing her cheek. 'Last minutes nerves about going to the West, I suppose. I can't thank you enough for arranging this. I don't know how you did it. I never thought it would be possible. The Romanian sculptor should be the one going. He's the artist, after all.'

'But you are the expert on his work. And from what you've said, he's reclusive.'

'That's true. Well. Goodbye, Marlis. Don't spend too much money while I'm away.'

She flung her arms around her husband and kissed him. 'Be careful, Kurt.'

'You worry unnecessarily, Marlis. What about I bring you a present? Some perfume perhaps?'

'Oh! I'd love that!' Marlis said.

Friedleman turned to Ivkin. 'Do you think such decadence is allowed?'

'I'm sure it will be fine. Besides, they won't know if we don't tell them.'

'You're a good friend, Grigori. I couldn't have done this without you. I'm still not sure how you arranged it. Contacts I suppose. I just wish you were coming too.' He bent to pick up his suitcase. 'Goodbye, Marlis. Take care.'

Kurt followed Grigori down the stairs and towards the waiting car. The driver got out and opened the door for the scientist, then, reaching for his suitcase, placed it into the boot.

'Grigori, I must speak with you,' Kurt whispered while the driver was attending to his luggage. 'I may be in trouble.'

'What is it?'

'You know I have a little book I keep beside my bed. In case I think of an idea during the night. I am positive I had it on my bedside table. Now I can't find it.'

Ivkin frowned. 'What was in it?'

'Thoughts. Random ideas. You know the sort of thing. I'm not a security risk, I promise you.' The driver returned and held the door for Ivkin.

'You know nothing is meant to leave the lab,' Ivkin whispered.

'No one would know what it's about, Grigori. They're just random sketches.'

Ivkin's frown deepened. He looked into the distance, aware that Friedleman was watching him. He nodded and smiled. 'I'm sure it will be fine. Besides, it's too late now to worry about it. Get in, Kurt or we'll be late for the crossing.'

'Of course. Thank you, Grigori.'

The car sped off, heading for Frontstadt.

Ivkin stared through the window at the endless grey stone buildings. On occasions, he flicked a glance at Friedleman. He could see the sweat building up on the man's upper lip as the checkpoint came into view. The car slowed.

'You'll be met in Paris by a driver from the Soviet Embassy there. This woman,' Ivkin reached into his coat pocket and withdrew a photo. He handed it to Friedleman. 'Her name is Irina Goskova.

'Can I keep this?'

'No, I have to return it. Memorise the face. You'll stay at the Soviet Embassy until your appointment with the Head Curator at the Louvre on Monday at ten, then you'll leave the next day. The same driver will take you to the airport. If you leave the embassy, for any reason, you will be accompanied. And, most likely, followed. Don't forget to buy the perfume.'

'You think I should?'

'Yes. It's a sign you're not defecting.'

Kurt's eyes widened. 'I wouldn't.'

'I'm pleased to hear it.'

In the distance, beyond all the barriers, and an area completely devoid of structures, Grigori could see the small hut where the American guards waited. One was already standing waiting for them, his hands wrapped around the machine gun in his grip, his helmet bright against the grey day.

'I'd be happier if you were coming with me.'

'Give me your papers, Kurt. Get out now but wait here by the car, I'll speak to the guards.'

Kurt's unsteady hand passed the papers to Ivkin. Leaving Friedleman standing beside the car, Ivkin walked towards the Soviet checkpoint hut a few feet away. He reached into his coat for his KGB security pass. Showing it to the guard, he walked inside as light rain began to fall. 'I need to use the telephone. And be quick about it.' Ivkin reached for the receiver and dialled the number for Stasi Headquarters. He glanced at the hovering guard, then decided to speak to his superiors in Russian. Replacing the receiver, he turned to the guard. 'One of you is to come with me and Herr Friedleman as far as the midpoint. Wait there. Only raise your weapon if you see me signal you. I will remove my scarf.'

The guard nodded. 'You suspect something, Comrade?'

'I suspect everything. Just do as you're told, and it will go as planned.'

Ivkin pulled up his coat collar as he returned to the car. Kurt hadn't moved from the side of the vehicle, his knuckles white from gripping his suitcase. 'The guard will walk with us to the halfway point. Good news, Kurt. I have permission to accompany you. It seems I'm coming with you after all.'

Kurt beamed. 'That's wonderful news! Thank you, Grigori. I don't know how you managed it. I feel so much better now.' He paused. 'But what about some clothing? You only have your work bag with you.'

'I'll get something there. It's only a few days. Shall we?' Ivkin gestured towards the barbed-wire festooned hedgehogs and the long, exposed road ahead. Above the Western hut, some hundred yards distant from where they stood, the American flag fluttered in the light breeze. But in the north, grey clouds were building; they foretold a dismal day ahead for Berlin. They walked slowly, weaving between the hedgehog barriers that segmented the road to the West, the East German guard following. Nothing was said.

Ivkin paused as they walked past the last hedgehog into no-man's-land. He scanned the road ahead for any sign of entrapment. Before them was a wide expanse of about twenty yards, the bitumen shining from the brief shower of rain, the road completely empty, devoid of barriers, buildings and guards. Nothing was there except the straight, exposed vastness. Its wide emptiness was a salient reminder that anyone crossing there was totally unprotected.

Ivkin turned to the guard. 'Wait here.' He shifted his focus to Friedleman. 'Kurt, I'll give our papers to the American guard. Better I answer any unexpected questions they may have in English.'

'If you think it best, Grigori. Lucky you speak so many languages. I'm so grateful for this. You are a loyal friend.'

They walked in silence towards the Western barriers as an American guard carrying a large machine gun in his grip stepped from the hut and waited beside it.

Ivkin glanced at Friedleman. The man's fear was palpable.

'Keep a steady stride, Kurt,' Ivkin said.

'I think I may faint.'

'Not a good idea. Take deep breaths.' Ivkin walked beside Friedleman as they wove their way around the western side hedgehog barriers towards the guard's hut.

Withdrawing the papers from his coat pocket, Ivkin held the young guardsman's gaze. 'Give these to the Officer in Charge.'

'Wait here, Sir,' the guard replied.

Even though now some distance behind them, Ivkin knew the East German guard would be watching, his finger resting on the weapon's trigger.

Three minutes passed. He could smell Friedleman's fear. Then the door to the American hut opened, and Ivkin saw the officer give the order to raise the final barrier. 'We can cross now, Kurt.'

'Is everything alright?' Kurt questioned, his voice shaking.

'Yes. Everything is as it should be.'

CHAPTER TWO

Leconfield House, MI5 Headquarters - London
Thursday 18th July 1968 - Afternoon

Jenkins stood in front of a mirror in the men's lavatory on the third floor. He straightened his tie, then pulled on his jacket. He did up the middle button, checked himself in the mirror, then undid it. Whichever way he fastened his coat, or sucked in his paunch, he knew he'd put on weight. He hoped the summons to the new Director General's office had nothing to do with fitness levels. He ran down the stairs to the first floor, a ridiculous attempt to remove a pound or two before standing before the discerning eye of Sir Giles Merrick-Smith. He nodded to Miss McKillick the loyal secretary to the last three Directors General of MI5, then knocked on the door.

'Come!'

Jenkins drew himself up, then opened the door and stood in front of his boss's desk. 'You wished to see me, Sir Giles?'

'Where is he?'

'Who, Sir?'

'Don't be obtuse, Jenkins. Alistair Quinn.'

'About forty thousand feet up, I should think, Sir.' Jenkins said with a smile. It faded. Quickly. His superior, Sir Giles Merrick-Smith, the recently appointed Director General of MI5 evidently didn't do humour. 'On his way home, Sir.'

'Good. As soon as he arrives, I want him in my office.'

'Something I should know about?'

Sir Giles looked up, his large ears like radar dishes. 'When I deem it appropriate.'

'I am his case officer, Sir Giles.'

Merrick-Smith stared at Jenkins, the eyes fixed, the expression resolute.

Jenkins saw the chin lift the thin lips into a hard line of annoyance.

'I am aware of that,' Merrick-Smith said.

'I'll send a car to the safe house in Knightsbridge to collect him, Sir. Just as soon as we get word he's arrived,' Jenkins added.

'Do that.' Merrick-Smith lowered his head, terminating the interview.

Jenkins left the plush first floor office and rode the lift to his dingy room on the top floor. Since Alistair's mother, now Dame Grace Quinn had relinquished the top job at MI5, Jenkins had never felt entirely comfortable with Merrick-Smith. Not that he'd ever felt at ease with Alistair's mother. While everyone at *Five* held her in the highest esteem, she had been a formidable taskmaster with a very short fuse. With the coming of the current Head of MI5, everyone there had hoped for a more agreeable demeanour from their boss. Merrick-Smith had been at MI5 a long time, since before the war, but his appointment as Head had surprised more than a few. His training as a solicitor had made him methodical and analytical. He was the total opposite to Dame Grace Quinn. It was said that Dame Grace had a nose that could sniff trouble through brick walls before it happened. Merrick-Smith wanted evidence before forming conclusions. And irrefutable evidence before taking action. Yet the man was not to be underestimated. Jenkins drew in a deep sigh. The previous ten years had been some of the worst in the agency's existence. The scandal of Philby et al. at MI6 had left them all chasing shadows. Some believed there was still a mole there. Or possibly at MI5. But since the death of Sir Laurence Dalrymple, life at Leconfield House had settled down. Merrick-Smith had seen to it. And the Americans didn't see them as bumbling idiots anymore. Sir Giles had, it had to be said, achieved the impossible.

Jenkins opened the door to his tiny space and sat behind his desk. It was a far cry from the plush offices and meeting rooms on the first floor. His workspace held an old wooden desk with a telephone, decrepit desk chair, one stained armchair, three filing cabinets and a low credenza with one small round window that allowed no view other than the sky. And all this luxury was contained within a tiny, cold space with a single overhead light and peeling paint. Sitting, he reached for the file on Alistair Quinn. Quinn's 'job' as an airline steward was the perfect cover for him. But Jenkins surmised he wasn't going to like what he would be doing first on return to London.

'Probably needed,' Jenkins muttered to himself. He leaned back in his chair, wondering why Sir Giles wanted Alistair so urgently. The compulsory medical would have to wait.

The door opened with a flourish, and Jenkins looked up.

Alistair stood in the doorway. Without speaking or waiting to be asked, he threw his pack on the floor, then slouched into the chair in front of Jenkins's desk. Crossing his long legs, he lit a cigarette.

Jenkins eyed Alistair's airline steward's uniform. 'Welcome home. I sent a car to Knightsbridge.'

'Really? As you see, I came here first.'

'Why?'

'Have something for you.' Alistair leaned forward and rested the cigarette on the ashtray on Jenkins's desk, then unzipped his bag and withdrew a large envelope.

'What is it?' Jenkins asked.

'How would I know. I carry them, I don't write them. Nor do I read them.'

'Who gave it to you?' Jenkins said, checking the seals on the A4 size envelope.

'Jenkins, as you well know, I collect instructions and mail from my post office box. That's all. So how would I know who it's from.'

Jenkins broke the seal and spent only two minutes reading the contents.

Alistair watched his case officer. The colour had rather rapidly drained from Jenkins's face, so much so that he seemed frozen in time. Alistair's gaze drifted to the skies beyond Jenkins's window. Blue. And sunny. He stood, stubbed out his cigarette and reached for the pack. 'Well, if that's it, I'll be off. I have a very nice afternoon planned.' Taking only two paces, he reached for the door handle.

'How's your mother?' Jenkins called.

Alistair turned, the question truly surprising him. 'Mother? Why do you ask?'

'Just wondered. She was our boss for a while.'

'To answer your question, she's fine. Although she's not fond of Australia. She lives with a friend now, a woman of her own age. I get the impression they've known each other for a while.'

Jenkins frowned. 'Really? Did you ask about this woman? She could be a risk.'

Alistair blinked. 'Would you?'

Jenkins leaned back in his chair. 'Perhaps not.'

'Well, I'll leave you with it,' Alistair said, turning towards the door again.

'Before you go! Merrick-Smith wants to see you. Now. Then when you've finished, you need to see the doctor.'

Alistair turned to face Jenkins, his lips pursed.

'It's just routine. The doctor, I mean. Just in case. Given your liking for the ladies. You understand.'

Alistair's puckered lips twisted into a grimace. He dropped his bag, then checked his watch. 'Everyone wants me today. Shame. I had planned to spend this afternoon with a delightful blonde from First Class. I don't expect our fearless leader wants me for the same reason.'

Jenkins's eyes had returned to the letter.

'I was joking about Merrick-Smith. I'm sure he's a happily married man.'

Jenkins looked up. 'What? Oh, yes. Let me know what he wants before you go?'

Alistair nodded. Collecting his bag, he closed the door and sauntered towards the stairs. He hoped that whatever Merrick-Smith wanted wouldn't take long. As he descended to the lower floors, his thoughts returned to Jenkins and his curious reaction to the contents of the envelope. He'd never seen the man so rattled.

Alistair stepped into the Director General's outer office. Miss McKillick looked up from her typing and beamed. He saw her eye course over his uniform. 'Very nice. It suits you,' she said. She inclined her head towards the closed door to the Director General's office. 'He's expecting you.'

Alistair winked at the efficient Miss McKillick, then tapped on the inner door.

'Come!'

He stepped inside.

Nothing much had changed in the Director General's office since his mother had occupied the chair. The large desk was still piled high with files. Perhaps the blue velvet curtains over the window behind Merrick-Smith's chair were new, but Alistair wasn't sure.

Sir Giles stood and walked around his desk. 'So, you're Alistair Quinn. I knew your mother, of course. And your father.'

'Better than I did, I suspect.'

'I was sorry to hear about his passing.'

Merrick-Smith held Alistair's gaze for a few seconds. But all Alistair saw was the man's enormous ears and the way the light from the window behind him made them appear bright red. Besides, he considered the manner of his father's death wasn't something for general discussion.

'It's difficult for the family,' Merrick-Smith went on. 'Too many secrets, I suppose. However, I hear you did a highly successful job with him a few years ago,' the Director General said then resumed his seat.

'That's right,' Alistair said hoping Merrick-Smith would soon discontinue the topic.

Merrick-Smith pointed to the chair opposite his desk. Alistair sat as directed. He stared through the window to the blue sky beyond. Any discussion of his late father always had the same effect; images of a man he barely knew, and memories filled with loathing and doubt. And all welded together with the instant and nauseating reminders of childhood beatings infused with the smell of cigarette smoke. While his boss shuffled files, Alistair twisted the signet ring on his little finger, the family motto *Neither Despise Nor Fear* engraved on it, his mind momentarily dwelling on the night his father had given it to him.

'I'll get straight to the point. There is something I need you to do. Can you get leave from the airline?'

'Of course. They know what I do.'

'Do they ask questions?'

'Never. Whatever my mother arranged, they've abided by.'

'Good. Needless to say, what I'm about to ask you is so secret, you cannot tell anyone. Even Jenkins.'

Alistair stared at the man he had already nick-named *Big Ears*. 'Well?'

'It's a job for MI6, actually. We've been asked to do it because they want a complete unknown. They'd like you to make contact with someone. Earn his trust, you know the sort of thing. He's in Berlin currently. But we've had a tip off from the Americans that he'll be in Paris later today. Get close to him and find out what you can, who he meets and if possible, why he's really in Paris.'

'Do you have a picture?'

'No. But we do have a name. Kurt Friedleman.'

'His importance?'

'He's a scientist. But he's in Paris to promote the work of a Romanian sculptor. Apparently, he's an expert on the artist. He hopes to persuade the French to exhibit the work in the new Paris Art Museum.'

'If you don't know what he looks like, how sure are you this tip-off is genuine?'

'Crossed the border this morning through the American sector. And he's not using an alias. It's possible he's working on something that could give the Soviets the advantage for the next decade. His visit to Paris could be completely innocent. But given his area of expertise it's unlikely.'

'And that is?'

'Radar.'

'I'm surprised the Soviets let him come to the West.'

'So are we. But he isn't alone. He has a KGB colonel with him. Regardless, you don't have long to gain his trust. He's only in Paris a few days.'

'Is it possible he wants to defect?'

'Unknown.'

'What's he working on specifically?'

'Also unknown.'

'Radar's rather old technology, isn't it?'

'Not at all! And certainly not if he's invented something new.' Merrick-Smith reached for a sealed envelope. 'This is important, Quinn. If our suspicions are correct and he's invented an early warning system for the Soviets to know if a ballistic missile has been fired, they have a worrying advantage over us. It's vital we know what his intentions are and, if possible, what he's invented.' Merrick-Smith placed the envelope on the desk in front of Alistair. 'Airline tickets and accommodation for you in Paris are in here along with some maps of Paris and the locations of the Soviet embassy and our own.'

'Where's he staying?'

'Soviet Embassy.'

Alistair let out a burst of air. 'Wouldn't someone more senior than me be better for this? I mean, how do you expect me to meet him much less get to know him in a few days sufficient to earn his trust, especially if he's holed up in the Soviet Embassy? They'll be watching him day and night.'

Merrick-Smith swivelled his chair. 'I realise it's a tall order, Quinn, but I'm told you're inventive. Use it. And your intuition. Besides, MI6 want an unknown, and you have some necessary skills. You speak Russian for one thing, and I'm informed, you have a way with the ladies.' Merrick-Smith looked Alistair in the eye. 'He'll be met at the airport by a young woman from their embassy who seems to meet all incoming Soviet guests. This woman.' Merrick-Smith handed Alistair a photograph. 'Her name is Irina Goskova.' Merrick-Smith went on. 'I'm sure you've heard the rumours. After the Philby disaster, some here and at MI6 still suspect an undiscovered mole. One that may not even be in London but someone who has a high security clearance and has access to classified information. You see our concern. Leaks of any kind are problematic. But leaks at a high level are catastrophic. And an unknown person could do some discrete digging without drawing too much attention their way. No one would question your involvement for this level of assignment.'

'So, I'm the scapegoat?'

Merrick-Smith sat upright, his left eyebrow rising almost imperceptibly. 'There are always inherent dangers in our line of work.'

Alistair studied Merrick-Smith's face. Yes, he thought, but they're usually from the other side, not your own.

'You have less than five days to learn whatever you can by whatever means. I realise, Quinn this assignment will be difficult, but time is against us, and we have no alternative. If further action is required, you can contact me either through our embassy in Paris or by my direct telephone line. The number is in the envelope. Check in with them regularly in case we have any further instructions for you. Then, come and see me on return.'

Alistair stood. Closing the door to Merrick-Smith's office, he winked to Miss McKillick. Even though she was on the telephone, she beamed up at him as he passed.

'Early flight to Paris, please,' Miss McKillick said into the telephone receiver. 'Leaving tomorrow morning. Just the one passenger. In the name of Patrick Scully.'

Alistair frowned as he let himself out of the office. Patrick Scully. He knew the name was an alias MI5 had used once before. Outside, he opened the envelope and quickly flicked through the contents. He reached immediately for the airline ticket. He was booked on the ten a.m. flight to Paris. The ticket was in the name of Simon Cordery, Art Historian. The other documents could wait until he was in his room at the safe house.

Not being able to speak with Jenkins was unusual and made his task more difficult. But Merrick-Smith hadn't said anything about Jenkins finding him an artist and a scientist to quiz about Romanian sculptors and the latest developments in radar. Climbing the stairs, he returned to Jenkins's office on the top floor.

'What did he want?' Jenkins asked, looking up as Alistair flopped into the chair.

'Can't say. Who's the top scientist around at the moment?'

'Curious question. I'll find out. I imagine you want to pick his brains.'

'No. I thought we could chat about fish quotas.'

Jenkins smirked. 'I'll arrange it. Anything else?'

'I also need to talk to someone from the National Gallery about modern sculpture.'

Jenkins's eyebrows shot up. 'Right! What time tomorrow?'

'It'll have to be tonight.'

'Bloody hell!' Jenkins let out a long sigh. 'I'll pull a few strings.' Jenkins paused. 'And Alistair. Whatever Merrick-Smith wants you to do, stay in England, would you?'

'Why?'

'Just do as you're told for once.'

Outside Alistair stood on the curb and waited for a break in the traffic before crossing. He cut through Shepherd's Market to Piccadilly. The daylight was fading, the gentle summer evening light settling on the trees in Green Park. Waiting only minutes, he hailed a cab outside the Ritz. He settled back and stared at the streets of London as they headed for the safe house in Knightsbridge. But his mind was on Jenkins, or *Three Piece Suit* as he'd once nick-named Jenkins. But that was three years ago. Then their relationship was different. Almost master and servant. Now, he wasn't the boy MI5 had recruited in Soho anymore. Now he and Jenkins were almost equals. He imagined Jenkins sitting in his tiny office pouring over files. Or one envelope especially. Alistair frowned recalling Jenkins's parting words to him. Why had Jenkins asked him to stay in Britain? Although it hadn't been said as a direct order. Alistair inhaled deeply. Regardless, *Big Ears* out-ranked Jenkins, so *Three Piece* would just have to live with it. Alistair reached into his coat pocket for his cigarette case and taking one out, lit it. What were his bosses up to, keeping things from each other? He found the idea of spy masters keeping secrets from each other rather amusing. But what was Merrick-Smith hiding from his subordinates? And why? Alistair gazed at the London traffic, then closed his eyes. There were no answers to those questions. At least, not yet. He drew in a long breath through his nose then stifled a yawn. He was tired. They'd had a few difficult passengers onboard the Heathrow flight, and he needed a drink, food and sleep, in that order. But with a scientist and an art expert to see he was in for a long night. And his date with the blonde from First Class was now nothing more than a dream.

He jumped from the cab in Brompton Road and walked to the underground car park, the secret and only access into the MI5 safe house. Once inside, he took the stairs to Room 39, his room since his first visit to the house in 1965. In the corner of his small room was the silk robe on a stand and a pair of slippers beneath the chair. His jeans and black leather coat hung in the wardrobe. Everything the same. His eye caught the unopened bottle of whisky on the table in the corner. He smiled. He suspected Dorothy, his maid, had placed it there once she'd been alerted to his imminent arrival. 'Thank

God for Dorothy,' he muttered, then un-corked the bottle and poured some into a crystal glass. He took two long sips, then opened his wardrobe and changed his clothes, hanging his uniform carefully in the cupboard. Once seated in the armchair and with the glass of whisky in one hand, he opened the envelope *Big Ears* had given to him. Other than the airline ticket, it included a map of Paris, a hotel voucher and two smaller sealed envelopes. He tore one open. It held a thousand pounds in French francs. The cash and the hotel voucher he put into his coat pocket along with the airline ticket. He then spread the map out on the bed and noted the locations of his allotted hotel and its distance to the British Embassy in Rue du Faubourg St Honoré and the Soviet one some miles away in Boulevard Lannes. It was nowhere near the British Embassy or the nearby American Monolith in Avenue Gabriel. In fact, Alistair considered, the two great Western powers' embassies were so closely located, they doubtless had underground tunnels for ease of communication. He reached for the other sealed envelope and withdrew a single page document, along with the photograph of Irina Goskova. He smiled. She was attractive. Blonde hair with wide blue eyes and a flawless complexion. She was older than him but not by much. Just the way he liked it. He placed the photograph on the small table, the pretty face staring back at him. He poured another whisky then sat again to read the note.

Friedleman is approximately fifty-five with short brown hair. He wears tortoiseshell rimmed glasses and is approximately five feet eight inches tall. His meeting with the Head Curator, M. Benoit Lebec is at the Louvre next Monday at ten. He's staying at the Soviet Embassy but will be collected at the airport most probably by Irina Goskova (photograph supplied).

Alistair reached again for the photograph, his mind on how he could meet her. She, he hoped, would be his entrée into meeting Friedleman. But how to bring it about? 'Take risks, Quinn,' he muttered. He'd never been averse to that.

An hour passed before the anticipated call from Jenkins during which time, Alistair ate dinner in his room.

The telephone rang as he sipped the last of his whisky.

'Professor Lloyd will see you here,' Jenkins said. 'I've sent a driver to collect him from Oxford, so he should be here about half past eight tonight. You can use the meeting room on the third floor.'

'Good evening to you, too, Jenkins.'

Jenkins didn't respond.

'And the art expert?'

'He'll meet you here, too. Same place. At ten.'

'Right!'

'Alistair,' Jenkins paused. 'Something I should know about?'

'No.' Alistair hung up. He knew Jenkins would be more than curious, but until Merrick-Smith said otherwise, no one was to know.

He heard the light click as his bedroom door opened a crack. 'Hello, Sir,' the soft female voice behind him said.

Alistair turned. 'Dorothy. Good to see you.'

'And you, Sir. Staying long?'

'Just tonight. And thank you for dinner and the whisky.'

'Pleasure.' Her eyes went to the bottle on the table which was now almost empty. 'Can I get you some tea?'

Alistair laughed. 'You read my mind, Dorothy.'

CHAPTER THREE

Paris

Thursday 18th July 1968 – Afternoon

Ivkin had insisted Friedleman take the window seat in the aeroplane. He knew the man would want to see the city of Paris as they descended, but he had his own motives. Friedleman couldn't leave his seat or converse with other passengers while Ivkin occupied the aisle seat. But it hadn't stopped the flight from being tedious. Not from turbulence or loud, disagreeable passengers or even bad service but from Friedleman's own inexperience and awkwardness. The man's anxiety was palpable. He'd sat almost motionless for the entire journey with what Ivkin recognised as fear. Not fear of flying, although Ivkin knew Friedleman had never flown before, but a fear that came from apprehension, the anticipated trepidation of the unknown. Too terrified even to go to the toilet onboard until Ivkin reassured him nothing would happen to him.

Ivkin preceded Friedleman down the stairs and across the tarmac into the terminal building.

'Do you know where we have to go?' Friedleman asked.

'Yes. Keep up, Kurt.'

They walked with other passengers along narrow linoleum corridors until they entered the wide Immigration area where customs men sat on elevated daises ready to scrutinize faces and passports. Friedleman's expectant expression constantly roamed around the hundreds of queueing noisy passengers all waiting to pass through the barriers. Ivkin glanced at him. Perhaps Friedleman expected to be detained. Perhaps the whereabouts of his missing notebook still played on his mind.

'Have you been to Paris before, Grigori?'

'Yes. Relax, Kurt. You worry too much. Our driver will be outside to take us to the embassy.' Ivkin stepped forward and handed his East German Diplomatic Passport to the immigration official. Friedleman stood behind him, but Ivkin could feel Friedleman's penetrating gaze.

'How long are you staying in France?' the official asked Ivkin.

'Five days.'

The customs officer stared into Ivkin's eyes. 'The purpose of your visit?'

'Diplomatic business.'

The immigration official examined his face, shrugged, then stamped the passport. Ivkin walked through the barrier and loitered on the other side. Bending, he pretended to tie his shoe-lace as Friedleman stepped forward and handed his passport to the French official.

'Another East German! How long are you staying in France?' the official asked Friedleman.

'Till Monday next,' Friedleman answered.

'Your purpose in coming to France?'

'I have an appointment with Monsieur Lebec, Head Curator at The Louvre. I have papers...' Friedleman reached into his coat.

The customs officer stared at Friedleman with no hint of a smile. A few moments passed before he stamped the passport and handed it back. 'Welcome to Paris.'

Friedleman pushed the papers into his coat then joined Ivkin on the other side of the immigration cubicle.

'Where do I collect my luggage?'

'Not far. They may want to inspect your suitcase.'

'What for?'

'Alcohol. Cigarettes. Even furs. Do you have anything in your suitcase other than clothes?'

'No. Just my clothes and some notes for the meeting.'

'Nothing to worry about then. This way, Kurt,' Ivkin said, pointing to a sign that indicated the way to the baggage area in the Paris International Airport. They walked for some time along more linoleum covered corridors, then finally into a large open space where long rows of suitcases were lined up on trolleys. Beside each were two men, checking off names before any luggage could be taken away.

'I'm so pleased you're with me, Grigori. I wouldn't know where to go or what to do,' Friedleman said, his eyes darting around the busy terminal.

Ivkin walked towards the trolleys and reached for a brown leather suitcase and set it down beside him. 'Is this it?'

'Yes. Yes, this is it. Marlis stuck a stamp on the outside near the handle so I could recognise it.'

'Good idea,' Ivkin said. 'And Kurt, keep an eye on your luggage. There are thieves and pickpockets in the West.'

'Really? Are we safe?'

'Just be mindful of who is around you.'

Friedleman gripped the handle of his suitcase. 'Are there any more authorities?'

'No. We are free to leave.'

Ivkin glanced sideways. Friedleman's shoulders had visibly dropped with relief. But the idea of total freedom was a concept unknown to Friedleman. The door opened automatically, and they walked together into an area where people stood waiting to welcome family and friends.

Grigori Ivkin loved Paris, and he was eager to see it again. Everything about the place pleased him. Especially in spring and summer: the warm gentle air, the bright flowers, their joyful colours and pleasant fragrance, the blue hue of the city, the pretty girls and the heady French tobacco. Not to mention the strong coffee served by waiters wearing long white aprons, waistcoats and bow ties. Parisiens whether male or female had an air of indifferent sophistication. And rules seemed only to exist to be ignored. Ahead he recognised from the photograph their contact, Irina Goskova. She was older than he'd expected from the photograph with a head of long blonde hair. She wore blue stiletto heels that would never have been purchased in Moscow or East Berlin. Ivkin walked towards her and kissing her checks, introduced Kurt.

'You know Comrade Goskova?' Kurt whispered to him.

'We've never met. It is customary in France to kiss both cheeks on greeting friends. Everything must look correct.'

They walked out of the building into the morning sunlight, the sky a gentle almost soporific blue. Near the taxi rank, a black car with darkened windows was parked by the curb. As soon as Irina walked towards it, the engine started.

'Sit in the back with Comrade Goskova,' Ivkin said walking around the car to sit in the front with the driver. Friedleman did as instructed.

The car pulled away from the curb and joined the traffic heading into the city.

'The Soviet Ambassador is out this afternoon,' Goskova said. 'But you're both invited to join him tomorrow evening for drinks. We are holding a reception for the new Swedish Ambassador. There will be some notable local dignitaries present. I understand M. Lebec is also invited. Our ambassador is keen to hear about the sculptor you so admire Herr Friedleman.'

Friedleman seized the opportunity to tell Goskova all he knew about the artist. Ivkin stared through the window. He'd heard it all before.

The car swung into the Soviet Embassy compound, the gates closing behind them. To Ivkin's eyes, it was the ugliest building he'd ever seen and resembled a giant, inverted toast rack. In his opinion, it was completely out-of-place in a city of such architectural beauty. Irina Goskova was the first to get out. 'If you'll follow me, I'll show you to your rooms. Then after, I'll show you around our embassy. Not everywhere, of course, but perhaps you would like to see our art collection and the public spaces.'

'I need to purchase some clothes this afternoon, Comrade Goskova,' Ivkin said. 'As I'm sure you know, my presence here was only arranged at the last minute. Herr Friedleman can join you on the tour, then he should spend some time going over his notes for his meeting on Monday.'

'As you wish, of course. However, Major Boyanski, our resident KGB officer is eager to meet you, Comrade Ivkin.'

'This evening. Perhaps.'

Ivkin followed Goskova through a side entrance and into the fortress-like embassy. Like most modern buildings the world over, there was a surfeit of grey concrete with slightly bizarre artworks designed to impress. But the back stairs areas were utilitarian only. Goskova left them on the third floor.

'Grigori, should I come with you this afternoon and buy the perfume?' Kurt asked.

'After Comrade Goskova has shown you around, you should spend some time on your presentation, then get some rest. Monsieur Lebec may quiz you tomorrow evening, and you must have all the answers to his questions. We'll get the perfume later.'

'Of course. Grigori?'

'Yes?'

'Is everything alright?'

'Why do you ask?'

'Why would a KGB officer be keen to meet you? Are you in trouble?' Friedleman paused, then whispered. 'Did you tell them about my notebook?'

'Of course, I haven't. Besides, this KGB officer would want to see you, not me, if that were the case.'

'Yes. You're right. But why would a KGB major want to see you? I thought you were a clerk at Stasi Headquarters.' Friedleman frowned. Ivkin held Friedleman's gaze. He saw the briefest, unspoken shift in Friedleman's expression where caution begins to swing from trust to doubt. 'Are you telling me that you're not a clerk at Stasi Headquarters?'

'I am a clerk, Kurt, but sometimes I'm asked to do other things.'

'May I ask what?'

Ivkin held Friedleman's intense gaze. 'You know I cannot answer that, and you shouldn't ask. After all I've done to get you here, Kurt, I think your suspicions both unworthy and unwarranted. But I will tell you this much. I came twice with a delegation. As a clerk, to record the meetings. Kurt, it's alright. You don't need to worry. Just get some rest and go over your notes.'

'Now I know how you live on the Majakowski Ring.'

'You are letting your unfounded suspicions get away with you, Kurt. I haven't lied to you. I am a clerk, but as I said, sometimes I'm asked to do other things.' Ivkin paused, the doubt on Friedleman's face still evident. 'I shouldn't be telling you this, but sometimes I'm asked to carry things to other countries. Now, don't ask me anymore questions or we'll both be in trouble.'

Friedleman paused. 'Does Ludmilla know?'

'She knows enough to keep her mouth shut. And so should you. If my superiors learn of your notebook, it would see you charged with espionage, if not shot. Or at the very least sent to Siberia. And there would be a similar fate for me for not informing them of it if they discovered I knew about it.'

Friedleman nodded. He licked his dry lips. 'Of course. I'm sorry Grigori. You're a good friend. I shouldn't have questioned you.' He paused, then leaned towards Grigori. 'Are we safe here?'

'The Soviet Embassy is about the safest place in the world for you. Stop worrying, Kurt. Relax, enjoy yourself. You might as well, you may never come here again.'

Ivkin watched Friedleman walk along the corridor to his allotted room. Friedleman's suspicions worried Ivkin but, he reasoned, at least they'd been voiced with him and not Boyanski or the ambassador. For now, he believed he'd quashed Friedleman's doubts, and the subject was unlikely to be raised again.

Leaving his briefcase in his room, Ivkin walked along the corridor to the bathroom. Inside he checked he was alone. He glanced around the small room. There was one window, slightly ajar. Standing beside it, he stared into the garden below. Several large trees filled the back on the embassy grounds, and a high wall separated the building from the side street. Below him was a sheer drop of about thirty feet to the concrete path.

He heard the door open.

'Colonel Ivkin?'

He looked up. Before him was a tall, not unhandsome man with a thick head of dark hair and the darkest brown eyes Ivkin had ever seen on a Russian. 'I am Major Michail Boyanski.'

Ivkin shook the proffered hand of the KBG officer.

'I am very pleased to meet you, Comrade Ivkin. Your reputation for thoroughness is legendary in the KGB.'

'Perhaps you will allow me to continue our discussion at another time and location. Men's lavatories are not the most congenial places for introductions.'

'Of course, Comrade Colonel. My apologies.'

'Oh, and Boyanski. My presence here in Paris was arranged at the last moment, so I need to purchase some clothing. While I am away this afternoon, keep an eye on Friedleman.'

'You have concerns?'

'I always have concerns. We are in Paris, not East Berlin. And the temptations are many.'

'He will be watched.'

Ivkin left the bathroom and returned to his room. Opening his wash bag, he withdrew an old, empty blue and white plastic *Tesco* bag. He pushed it into his coat pocket. Leaving the embassy by the front door, he crossed the lawn then showing his pass to the guard on the gate, walked out onto the road.

CHAPTER FOUR

Paris

Thursday 18th July 1968 – Evening.

Ivkin strode away from the Soviet Embassy. He heard the automatic gate behind him slam shut. On the opposite side of the street, he waited next to a bus stop that would take him to the Champs-Élysées and Paris's shopping district. He stood facing the oncoming traffic, as though trying to see the approaching bus. But his eye was on the Soviet Embassy perimeter fence. It was tall, about fifteen feet in height and made of single black metal poles cemented into the ground, with crossbars only at the bottom and at the top. No crossbars existed along the middle of the fence permitted for a foothold, and spikes were placed on the top of each pole. Neither were there any trees or shrubs planted along the boundary. A large bullet-proof, glass-fronted guards' hut stood just inside and beside the automatic front gate. Surveillance cameras peered down on the entrance from poles erected inside the embassy fence. Ivkin understood the embassy's appearance was not so much designed to keep people out, which, of course, it did, as much as it was to withhold those within. It was exactly as it appeared, unwelcoming and intimidating. Doubtless, Ivkin thought exactly what Moscow Central Committee had designed. For anyone who so desired, getting in or out, especially in daylight, had to be done via the normal channels. Roving cameras were also placed in prominent places around the fortress-like building. Surveillance cameras were, of course, standard procedure for most embassies, but his eye searched for hidden devices, those secreted in trees or at concealed and vulnerable points along the building. To Ivkin's trained eye, the building had been designed specifically to avoid vulnerability; it was impregnable. And escape proof. If someone wished to escape, it would be by audacity not stealth. And, he considered, Kurt Friedleman had neither.

As the bus pulled away from the curb, Ivkin checked his watch. His departure would have been recorded. He surmised he had approximately three hours before anyone took any interest in his whereabouts.

Alighting from the bus on the Champs-Élysées, Ivkin crossed the wide street several times, standing outside shops, window shopping, then entering larger stores via the front and exiting by a side door. In one, he bought a pair of jeans and some trousers, in another two white shirts, and in a third some underwear and a pair of sandshoes. Discarding one of the store bags into a suitcase on display in the travel section of the last department store, he returned to the street then crossed the Seine at Pont Alexandre III. Hurrying along the left bank he crossed again at Pont Neuf, to walk along the exclusive Rue de Rivoli. Opposite the Hôtel de Ville, he found a public convenience and descending the steps, entered a cubicle. Fifteen minutes later, a man wearing sandshoes, jeans and a white shirt and sporting a full beard with unkempt hair, left the underground lavatory. He carried a blue and white *Tesco* supermarket bag and walked with a limp. Making his way back towards the Louvre, he entered a tobacconist where he purchased a packet of *Gitane* cigarettes, some razor blades and a copy of the latest *National Geographic*.

***

Alistair sat in a meeting room on the first floor of Leconfield House, a glass of whisky and a packet of *Sobranie* cigarettes on the table beside him. He checked his watch. A few minutes after eight. His right hand played with the cigarette packet beside him, flipping it between his fingers. Finally, he took one out and lit it. Standing, he walked to the window and looked down on the street three floors below. The long twilight had commenced its gradual descent, and the evening air had taken on its translucent softness. Several lights were on in the windows of the building opposite. Below him, a car drew up beside the front door to Leconfield House, and an elderly man alighted. Alistair twisted the signet ring on his left little finger and returned to his seat under the stern-faced portrait of the first head of the Secret Service, Captain Sir Mansfield George Smith-Cumming KCMG CB. Five minutes later, Alistair heard the sharp single knock at the door. He drained the whisky glass then stood. 'Come in!'

The door opened, and a man of advanced years stood before him. The intense grey eyes flowed over the room finally settling on Alistair.

'Lloyd, here,' the elderly man said. 'I'm to see someone named Quinn?'

'Thank you for coming,' Alistair said. 'Whisky?'

'Don't mind if I do. You're Quinn?' Lloyd asked, taking in Alistair's jeans and black leather coat or perhaps it was his youthful appearance.

'I am. Don't let the clothes deceive you.' Alistair poured two whiskies and handed one to the professor.

'Thank you. My apologies. How can I help?'

Alistair indicated the chair beside his. 'By telling me everything you know about recent advances in radar technology?'

'Oh! Fascinating! How long do we have?' the man said, sitting. He sipped the single malt whisky, his eyes glowing with excitement.

Physics had never made sense to Alistair, but then he had paid little attention to the subject while at school. In fact, he'd not paid much attention to anything at school except operating his clandestine business with his old school chum under the nose of the headmaster, Doctor Petit. Professor Lloyd was the classic academic type, and Alistair momentarily wondered if professors got discounts on tweed. The old man prattled on about physics, and radar in particular, recounting his experiences during the war with what was then considered cutting-edge technology.

'Professor?' Alistair interrupted.

'Eh?'

'As our time together is limited, perhaps you could confine your information to recent advances both here and in the Soviet sphere?'

The professor leaned back in the chair. 'Ah, well, here, I can inform you but in the USSR?' the professor shrugged. 'It would be most interesting to know what the Soviets are working on,' Lloyd said, never once looking at Alistair. 'Of course, the big threat since the end of the war is over-the-horizon radar.'

'What's that exactly?' Alistair asked.

Lloyd placed his glass on the table between them, then leaned forward, his arms resting on his knees. 'Most interesting. Technically possible but...' he glanced at Alistair. 'I'm talking about advanced warning systems. Of a ballistic missile launch. Difficult, of course, and quite revolutionary. It would have to be on a huge scale. Expensive. Perhaps too expensive to consider seriously.' The professor chortled, but Alistair knew it was only for himself. 'In fact, the antenna would have to be massive.' The professor's eyes had glazed over. He suddenly sat up, then turned to Alistair. 'Of course. Silly of me!' He raised his right index finger and tapped his nose. 'How to keep something so big secret? That's the real question, isn't it?' The professor didn't wait for a reply. 'There'd have to be lots of empty, flat countryside. Well-nigh impossible in Britain with a village around every corner. But in the vast Steppes of the

USSR…' Lloyd's voice trailed off. The old man's expression told Alistair that his mind was elsewhere.

Alistair stood. 'Well, thank you for your time, Professor. I won't keep you further. Thank you for coming all the way from Oxford. Just stand outside on the footpath. The driver will collect you. Safe journey back.'

'What? Oh! Yes. Thank you for the drink.' Lloyd stood and downed the last of the whisky before returning the glass to the side table. 'Hope I've been of use. Most interesting. Do keep me posted. If you can, dear boy. Yes. Well, I'll be off then.'

'Professor.'

'Yes?'

'Please remember, you cannot talk about our meeting to anyone. May I remind you that you have signed the Official Secrets Act. And our Security Services take breaches very seriously.'

'Yes, of course. Mum's the word.'

'Good night, Professor.' Alistair escorted him to the lift. He glanced up the stairwell to where he knew Jenkins was working late. Perhaps Jenkins hoped to see him before leaving for the night. Perhaps he was hoping Alistair would spill the beans over a late-night whisky. He glanced at his watch. The art expert, Gerard Martin-Wilcox, was due in minutes. Alistair returned to the meeting room and lit another cigarette. Through the open double doors, he heard the lift doors open. Minutes later, a thin man wearing an immaculate suit, a purple tie and matching pocket handkerchief entered the room and glided to the chair beside Alistair.

'Are you Quinn?' Martin-Wilcox said in an exaggerated public-school voice. A frown gathered on his public-school forehead, and a disdainful eye hovered over Alistair's clothing.

'Yes. I would like to know a little about a Romanian sculptor...'

'Oh! What a genius!'

'I haven't said his name yet.'

Martin-Wilcox rolled his eyes. 'No need. There is only one of note.'

While Professor Lloyd had been informative about physics, Alistair decided that Gerard Martin Wilcox was a prig and a bore. He was like a wind-up toy with his effusive descriptions of the Romanian sculptor's effortless lines and tactile smoothness.

At midnight, Alistair took the stairs to the street and hailed a cab in Audley Street. As the taxi made its way towards Knightsbridge, he mused on what he'd learned from both men especially old Lloyd. If Friedleman had discovered a way of learning in advance if a missile had been launched, no wonder Merrick-Smith wanted it kept secret. Especially if a mole really did exist in MI5. His mind turned to who it could be. He pondered if the Director General suspected Jenkins. Alistair thought it unlikely given Jenkins history and his involvement in the mission Alistair had done with his late father two years previously. Alistair stepped from the cab at the corner of Brompton Road and entered the secret MI5 safe house through the underground car park as usual. His head was pounding, and he had a rampant hunger. Opening the door to his room, he saw Dorothy had left a plate of sandwiches on the bedside table. Beside it was a jug of water and two aspirins.

'Bless you, Dorothy,' Alistair muttered.

CHAPTER FIVE

London

Friday 19th July 1968 - Morning

Alistair rose early and dressed. He hadn't been to Paris in years. He was ambivalent about the city, and although he'd had some wonderful times there, he never felt completely comfortable with the French or their capital. He felt there was something almost subversive about Paris. If London was a placid dog of advanced years that lay by the fire and welcomed all-comers, Paris was a pedigree cat, aloof and secretive. And his impressions of the city had been confirmed with the outbreak of the volatile student and union riots that had taken place there two months previously. Such emotional outpourings, especially of the political variety, were usually met in England with a conservative sneer if not outright disdain.

At exactly six o'clock, Alistair made his way to the underground car park and waited by the entry door. He saw a car approach, then stop. It was a Bentley. He raised his eyebrows. If it was for him, then it was a far cry from the blue Citroën he'd been shunted about in before. He looked behind him, but there wasn't anyone else leaving the safe-house currently. The car pulled up beside him, and the driver got out. 'Mr Simon Cordery?'

'Yes.'

'I'm here to take you to the airport, Sir.' The driver opened the rear door for Alistair, then took his suitcase and placed it into the boot before returning to his seat behind the wheel. Alistair sat in the rear. A moment later, the driver caught his gaze in the rear-view mirror. 'There's a packet for you, Sir, in the seat pocket.' Alistair reached for it. It was addressed to Simon Cordery. In it there was another passport with his photograph in the name of John Pevington, and a note. It had two entries: an address for a bar in Place de la Madeleine and the direct line telephone number for Merrick-Smith.

Alistair held the second passport and stared at the photograph of his face. Evidently Merrick-Smith thought he'd need it. So, the Director General anticipated trouble. Enough for him to have to leave France under a different identity. Alistair put the passport in his jacket pocket, his mind on his mission. Surely Merrick-Smith knew it would be almost impossible for him to meet the East German who reputedly was holed up in the Soviet Embassy. And completely impossible for Alistair to learn anything of value, especially about sensitive work. The East German would be on high alert to strangers asking questions. So, what was Merrick-Smith's real purpose in sending him to Paris? But what nagged his mind more was why Jenkins had told him to stay in Britain.

***

East Berlin – same time

Marlis Friedleman heard the loud thumping.

'Open up!' The man's voice was harsh and loud.

She stared at the closed entry door to their flat, the fear rising. Drying her hands on a towel, she slowly approached her front door.

'Open this door or we'll smash it in!' the angry voice in the corridor outside shouted.

'Just a minute!' Marlis responded. She unbolted the lock and opened the door a crack. The door flew open, the angry man's boot splintering the timber jamb.

'What do you want?' Marlis demanded, backing away. 'My husband is away.'

'We know that!' The Stasi officer pushed Marlis into the chair in the sitting room. 'Sit there. And don't move!'

Three men then thundered along the hall; their weapons raised. Cupboards were being flung open, then drawers. Several times Marlis heard things being thrown on the tiled floor of the bathroom then the sound of glass shattering. The guard returned and stood over Marlis. 'Where is it?'

'I don't know what you're talking about,' Marlis said her voice quaking.

The guard reached forward, then swung the back of his hand across her face, making her cry out more in shock than pain. 'The notebook.'

'What...' she paused. 'His notebook. He kept it on the bedside table. Isn't it with him...?' she paused, her eyes wide in fright as the realisation of what she'd said struck. 'It must be here. He wouldn't have taken it to the West. Perhaps he left it at work? He's not a traitor, he's a patriot. If he has it, he's taken it by accident. He wouldn't betray the party. He wouldn't.'

The guard swung his machine gun over his shoulder.

'Nothing here, Captain,' one man called from the bedroom.

'Your husband will be arrested the moment he returns. If he returns. And when he does, you will notify us immediately. Immediately! Do you hear!' the guard shouted into her face then turned to the two other men. 'You've checked all cupboards and all the remaining clothes? And under the bed? What about the bathroom?'

'Yes, we've checked there too, Captain. It's not there.'

'Check the kitchen!'

Marlis heard the drawers and cupboards being flung open. Cutlery crashed to the floor as the drawers were emptied, and crockery was thrown onto the kitchen table. 'Nothing, Captain!'

The man scowled at Marlis. 'If you are hiding it for him, you will join him in the gulag.' He spun on his heel and left, slamming the door behind him.

Marlis stood trembling. Her heart was pounding. The shouting, the noise, the mess they'd left when they'd stormed into her house. In those few brief seconds, everything about her life was upended. She felt confused, and shock was quickly taking hold. She couldn't think. She felt faint. She reached for the armrest of her chair and sat again, staring into the air in front of her, her hands grasping her apron as the tears began to flow down her cheeks. Outside, she heard multiple car doors slam, then the sound of the engine fading as it drove away. Numb, she sat hardly able to breathe much less think. She began to shake as the confusion quickly turned into a mire of doubt. What did they suspect? Had Kurt done something? But where was the notebook, if not with him? How did they even know he had a notebook? What did they mean, *if* he returned. Had he defected? The thought terrified her. He wouldn't! He wouldn't leave her. It was unthinkable. There was no hint of it in his behaviour towards her. Yet, she recalled he was distracted yesterday morning when he'd left for Paris. She fell back in the chair. Fear gripped her and a sense of growing disbelief. She reached into her apron pocket for a handkerchief as tears of fear dripped from her cheeks and sobs became shrieks. Then betrayal. Had he left her? He would know the authorities would come to interrogate her. How could he do it to her? She shook with trepidation. Slowly she raised her hand to her aching face, the stinging pain numbed by the hollowness of suspected duplicity. Frowning, she tried to recall every detail of the previous morning. He'd been anxious before leaving. She'd thought it was nerves. About going to the West. Slowly she stood and checking the street first for anyone watching the apartment building, she reached for the telephone, her fingers shaking as she dialled the number.

'Ludmilla? It's Marlis. I need to speak to Grigori urgently.'

'Are you alright, Marlis?'

'I've just had a visit from...' she paused then whispered, 'the Stasi.'

There was silence for a few seconds. 'He isn't here, Marlis. I got a telephone call yesterday morning from Grigori's people. He's gone with Kurt to Paris. They'll be back on Tuesday. Don't worry so much. If Grigori is with him, he'll be fine.'

***

London - midday

Merrick-Smith turned his chair to face the window. Something troubled him. His feeling of unease was an unfamiliar sensation. Why had Bill Trant, Head of MI6 asked for an unknown to make contact with the East German scientist? And why had he asked MI5 to be involved? Was it because the mission to recruit the Soviet scientist was so secret that no one at MI6 was to know about it? Was it their intention to turn Friedleman to work for the SIS as a double agent or encourage him to defect? Was it a complete ruse to entrap a suspected mole in either service? He stared at the papers on his desk, but he wasn't looking at them. While he wasn't inclined to paranoia, he did wonder if they suspected him. Swivelling his chair, he lifted his gaze and stared into the morning sky, his hands gripping the armrests of his chair. He didn't like the feeling of being deliberately left in the dark. He needed information.

Merrick-Smith reached for the secure telephone and dialled the number for his counterpart at MI6. It rang only once.

'Trant.'

'Bill, it's Giles Merrick-Smith here. Can I have a word?'

'Of course, Giles. What's the problem?'

'This East German scientist, Friedleman.'

'What about him?'

'What are your intentions for him? And why did you want an unknown from MI5 to make contact?'

'I've told you why we want an unknown. Friedleman will be watched, so we can't use any of our people in case they're recognised. And I can't have our Soviet source compromised. If the Soviets got wind of our interest in Friedleman, they'd have him out of Paris quicker than you can say Jack Robinson.'

'And your intentions?'

'Well, it would be nice to know what he's working on.'

Merrick-Smith waited, but Trant didn't add anything further. 'So, it's not your intention to snatch him?'

There was a pause before Trant spoke again. 'If he'd been in London that may have been possible. Don't think the French would be too happy about us kidnapping a foreign national, especially an East German citizen, on their soil and whisking him out from under their noses. Not to mention how angry the East Germans would be. It would create a diplomatic incident with the French and the Soviets. We'll just wait and see what your fellow can discover. Who have you sent?'

'A newish lad. But from all reports, capable and has a degree of daring. Or so I'm told.'

'Aside from these attributes, does he have a name?'

'Alistair Quinn.'

There was silence at the end of the line. 'He's a bit young, don't you think. Maybe best to send someone more experienced.'

'Too late. He's already gone. Besides, I thought you wanted an unknown. What about your Soviet source, this chap with the odd code name. *Woodpecker*, Isn't it?'

There was a longer silence before Trant spoke again. 'Nothing we do must lead the Soviets to *Woodpecker*. Far too valuable.'

'And where is this *Woodpecker*?'

'Not sure. Could be anywhere.'

'You don't keep tabs on him?'

'Did I say our source is male?'

Merrick-Smith didn't answer.

'Giles, please understand, our Intelligence Officer is his own boss. And my choice of pronoun doesn't denote gender.'

'Do you know *Woodpecker's* identity?'

Trant didn't answer.

Merrick-Smith waited. He heard the line disconnect. A frown creased his brow as he replaced the telephone receiver. If Trant knew their source's identity, why wouldn't he share this information? It was more than annoying. He considered it downright offensive. Merrick-Smith leaned his left elbow on his desk and rubbed his forehead. He thought about Bill Trant. Trant had been at MI5 before becoming head of MI6 and was considered by many as the most senior man in both of the Services. In Merrick-Smith's opinion, this had made Trant arrogant. But was he hiding more than just their undercover agent's identity? The telephone call had brought more questions than answers. Merrick-Smith went over the conversation in his head. It was clear Trant suspected a mole. He'd said he didn't want anyone at MI6 to be recognised. Neither did he want a valuable asset to be compromised. Did that mean Trant believed the mole was in MI6, not MI5? Or was it that Trant thought young operatives at MI5 were expendable. Merrick-Smith shrugged. Truth was, it didn't matter if the intelligence officer was in MI5 or MI6, everyone was expendable.

Merrick-Smith leaned back in his chair and stared at the midday sky. Perhaps he should telephone the former Director General, Grace Quinn. She may know something and be more forthcoming. It was said she had a sixth sense for plots and double crosses. He chortled aloud. Ironic that it should be called a sixth sense. Almost as though *Six* was at the root of everything. He idly watched a cloud traverse his window. But a telephone call to Grace Quinn was out of the question. She'd retired. He visualised Grace Quinn's lined face and steely eyes. 'Tough old boot!' he heard himself mutter. He frowned. Perhaps he should have chosen someone other than Alistair for the job. If young Quinn got into trouble, or worse, wound-up dead, how would he explain it to the irate former Director General. Merrick-Smith lifted the telephone receiver and dialled the extension number for Jenkins. He heard it ring out. Rising, he walked to his office door. 'Miss McKillick, do you know where Jenkins is at present?'

'Not in his office, Sir?'

'He's not answering his telephone.'

'Of course. He isn't in, Sir. He was on this morning's early flight to Paris.'

'What! On whose orders?'

'I thought, yours, Sir Giles. He asked me to book his flight which I did.'

'When does he get back?'

'It was a one-way flight, Sir.'

CHAPTER SIX

Paris

Friday 19th July - Midday

Ivkin limped back along Rue de Rivoli, then sat in the Tuileries Gardens adjacent to the pond. Several children were playing with the model boats on the water. He pretended to watch them, but from the corner of his eye, he watched the adults in the park until he was satisfied no one was watching him. People came and went. Most were sitting in the metal chairs around the lake, or gathering around the garden beds, chatting, eating ice cream and enjoying life while their children played. Domesticity. It was as foreign a life to him as his would be to them. There, sitting among the naïve and the tourists, he put the clothes he'd purchased into one of the department store bags and put the blue and white *Tesco* bag in a nearby bin.

Ten minutes later, he walked towards the Place de la Concorde and crossing it, walked along the Champs-Élysées looking for the nearest entrance to the Metro. Once underground, he located the men's lavatory and removed the beard, combed his hair and changed his clothes again, leaving the shirt, jeans and sandshoes in a lavatory cubicle for the destitute of Paris to find.

Just before three, he strode through the gates of the Soviet Embassy, his newly acquired clothes in a bag. 'Is Major Boyanski available?' he asked the receptionist in the foyer.

'Of course, Comrade Colonel.'

Ivkin waited only minutes before Boyanski appeared. 'Please come to my office, Colonel Ivkin.' They left the entry foyer and walked down a hall that passed the central stairs to the upper floors. Boyanski's office was moderately large with modern minimalist furniture. On the wall opposite the man's desk were two portraits: one of Comrade Stalin and Comrade Khrushchev. Boyanski indicated the green vinyl chair, and Ivkin sat down. 'Would you like some vodka, Colonel?'

'It is too early for me.'

'Chia tea then?'

'I'm not here for a social chat, Boyanski. I wish to know about Herr Friedleman?'

'Comrade Friedleman spent an hour with Irina Goskova looking at the art here in the embassy. He then returned to his room where he has been ever since.' Boyanski paused, his gaze on the single bag of clothing. 'You didn't purchase much clothing, Colonel?'

'I bought some things. But I'm a simple man, Boyanski, a man of uncomplicated tastes who only needs a change of underwear and perhaps a clean shirt. I'm afraid I haven't, however, acquired a dinner suit for this evening's function.'

'I'm sure I can find you some appropriate attire. I'll see something is taken to your room.'

'Thank you.' Ivkin stood.

'Comrade Colonel?'

'Boyanski?'

Boyanski smiled. 'I would like to ask you about your career. It has been, how do they say it in the West, meteoric.'

'That is because I am thorough. Do you job well, Major. And you too will be noticed.' Ivkin walked to the door and let himself out.

Boyanski followed. 'Perhaps we can discuss your career this evening?'

'Perhaps. If you'll excuse me. I'd like to check on Herr Friedleman.'

'Of course.' Boyanski nodded.

Ivkin turned to climb the stairs, then paused and turned again, his gaze lingering on Boyanski who still stood at the foot of the stairs like a rottweiler awaiting his master's command. 'There are always positions for people who wish to be of service to our Mother Land. I'll make some enquiries for you on my return. Perhaps there is a position on my staff, if you would like that,' he said a broad smile spreading across his face. As he climbed the stairs, he could feel Boyanski's stare penetrating his back.

***

London

Merrick-Smith sat idly in his chair. He'd tried over the last few hours to focus on the mountain of paperwork on his desk, but his mind was elsewhere. The perplexing telephone call with Bill Trant was the cause. He wasn't sure what to make of it. Moreover, the knowledge that Jenkins had gone to Paris worried him. On whose orders? Suspicion was churning his gut. His right heel began to tap the blue carpet under his desk. In his mind, he went over every detail of the enigmatic conversation with Trant, but it yielded nothing he didn't already know. What was Trant concealing? Was there more to Trant's request for help? Surely Trant would know that five days to learn anything of value from the East German scientist was an impossibility. So what was MI6's real purpose? He didn't know. And Trant wasn't in any hurry to confide his true purposes. Even Jenkins's unexpected departure cast a suspicious shroud over events. He checked his watch, just after noon. Quinn would already be in Paris. He reached for the telephone and dialled the secure line for the British Embassy there.

'Sir Richard Greaves, please. Sir Giles Merrick-Smith speaking.'

Merrick-Smith waited.

'Sir Giles?'

'Greaves?'

'Yes, Sir. What can I do for you?'

'I've sent Alistair Quinn of our office to Paris on a job exclusively for me. I've asked him to check in with you regularly in case he needs assistance. He's young, Greaves, and while he has certain attributes for this job, he's not highly experienced. Could you get one of your people to keep an eye on him?'

'Of course. Anything of particular interest to you?'

'Only get involved if he's in trouble or if things get out of control.'

'Of course. Where is he staying?'

‘Hotel Nice in Rue Vignon.’

‘I know it.’

‘One more thing, Greaves. Do you know Andrew Jenkins of this office?’

‘Not personally.’

‘I want to know if he shows up at the Embassy.’

‘Anything else?’

‘No. Just keep me informed.’

Merrick-Smith hung up. He stroked his chin. Something was going on. He felt it.

***

The telephone was ringing.

‘Hello?’

‘Trant here. Thought you should know. I’ve just learned that Merrick-Smith has sent Alistair to Paris.’

‘What? We wanted a diversion not a catastrophe! Meddling fool!’

‘Alistair’s in over his head. Should we get him out?’ There was a long pause. Trant heard the long sigh at the end of the line. ‘What will you do?’

‘I’ll go myself.’

‘You think that wise?’

‘Wise or not. There’s no alternative now.’

CHAPTER SEVEN

Paris

Friday 19 July 1968 – Mid Afternoon

Alistair threw his suitcase onto the bed, then turned to survey the dingy room. The Hotel Nice was far from palatial. His room was accessed via a minute lift into a narrow corridor that looped back on itself then up sixteen steps. Any tourist guide would describe it as two stars at best. His room had dark wallpaper with strange exotic birds that appeared to loom over the bedhead. Guaranteed to give the occupant nightmares. On the opposite wall was a small closet, a narrow table, and just enough space to walk past the bed to look out the window into the street below. The view was far from exciting. Moreover, his room was not constructed for guests who were more than six feet tall. It was built into the mansard roof cavity. It had a bathroom, and squashed beside it and adjacent to the door was the top of the lift shaft, making it even more cramped. While he hadn't expected anything like the hotels on the Rue de Rivoli, he considered the Hotel Nice had seen little improvement in the twenty years since the end of the bloodiest conflict the world had ever experienced. He stepped into the bathroom, his head to one side to avoid hitting it on the sloping ceiling and turned on the tap over the basin. Murky brown water flowed from it. He then used the lavatory, pulling the long chain hanging from the ceiling to flush it. The same brown water sluggishly dribbled into the pan. At least it worked.

Unpacking his suitcase, Alistair placed his clothing into the wardrobe, then with his head bent to one side, he stood beside the flat top of the lift-shaft and spread the map of Paris out over the filthy red carpet covering. His eye coursed over the myriad of Parisien streets, his gaze again on the British Embassy and the Soviet equivalent. He wanted to see them. It was already mid-afternoon, and pedestrians and traffic, especially on the main thoroughfares, would be building up in readiness for the end of the working day. Leaving his cramped room, he descended to the street. Taking the cross street, he walked into Place de la Madeleine. Cars, lorries and motorcycles squeezed and wove their way around the imposing Church of La Madeleine at break-neck speed. Keeping to the narrow footpath, he walked past several flower sellers in green wooden shacks beside the magnificent edifice pondering how he was going to meet the East German. 'First things first,' he muttered to himself. Off to his right, he saw the bar Merrick-Smith had told him about and from where he could collect parcels without questions being asked. It was a double-fronted café bar with large red awnings covering the tables and chairs on the footpath. It looked innocuous enough. As he walked past it, he stared through the window. The interior appeared to be completely tiled, walls, columns and floor. A long wooden bar was to one side. It was superbly dark. No one outside could witness who met with whom or what the barman did. As much as he would have liked a drink, he continued on. Dodging the unforgiving traffic, he crossed the large square making for Rue Royale, then Rue du Faubourg St Honoré. Without loitering, he strode past the British Embassy. It looked exactly as he imagined, old, established, and with a commanding street presence. In fact, the large green double doors were reminiscent of a prison for the well-heeled. It was, however, the epitome of nineteenth-century Britishness in a foreign land; large, dominant and authoritative. He found himself smiling. Whether buildings or people, Alistair believed that such façades were nearly always designed to intimidate or, perhaps, disguise another agenda. Having sighted the British Embassy, he returned to the Madeleine and hailed a passing cab, giving the driver an address two blocks away from the Soviet Embassy. The taxi drove at speed along the Champs-Élysée.

Half an hour later, Alistair stepped from the cab near the entrance to a school. He then walked along Boulevard Lannes and stood beside the bus stop opposite the imposing Soviet Embassy. Its concrete enormity loomed over the passers-by. He thought it about as opposite an architectural style from the Soviet Embassy in London as could be imagined. He also knew there would be no late-night clandestine ingress into this modern fortress. Unless he could legitimately gain access, his only hope of making contact with Friedleman would be on Monday at the Louvre. Or a chance encounter with the delightful Irina Goskova. As he watched, the gate opened, and a vehicle drove out. He stared at it as it joined the traffic heading east, back into the city. The stark blackness of the car and its windows told him it was official, slightly threatening and most probably bulletproof.

'I wouldn't if I were you,' a quiet voice said in Alistair's ear.

He spun around.

'I'm Murray. From the embassy.'

'Which one?' Alistair asked, his gaze taking in the man's appearance. Murray was tall and lean with a decided air of superiority gained from attending the right schools and universities. Alistair felt an instant dislike.

'Ours. Your master asked me to watch out for you. Just in case you get into trouble, I was to render assistance.' Murray beamed an obsequious smile. 'I wondered why at the time, but I see now they've sent a boy to do an experienced man's job. And I'm only speaking to you because you are totally out of your depth. You won't get in. But Sir Richard will.'

'Sir Richard?' Alistair asked.

'Cultural Attaché at our embassy.' Murray glanced around, his eye on the camera by the Soviet Embassy gate. 'We should leave. A bus is due momentarily.'

Alistair looked along the street as Murray hailed the approaching bus. He preceded Alistair onto the vehicle. 'Sit in front of me,' Murray said, taking a seat on the left. Alistair did as instructed. He wasn't sure about the man or his unctuous smile. But while he thought Murray too suave by half, he didn't like it that Merrick-Smith was having him watched. So, not just the scapegoat, now not trusted either, he thought.

'I'll get off one stop before you. Come to the embassy. We'll talk there,' Murray said then standing walked towards the front of the bus and waited for it to stop. Alistair saw him step down and walk away. In the few minutes he had before the bus arrived at its next stop, he wondered if he should do as Murray asked. He didn't even know if Murray was who he said he was. But if the man was from the British Embassy and really did have access to the Soviets, it was too good an opportunity to miss. Besides, since when had taking risks ever worried him. He pulled the photograph of Irina Goskova from his pocket and stared at the attractive face. 'Too good an opportunity, indeed,' he whispered. One way or another, he determined, he'd meet the alluring Irina Goskova. Alistair pulled the cord to alert the driver, then walked towards the front of the bus and waited for it to stop. Stepping onto the pavement, he sauntered along the street and through a side garden that backed onto the British embassy and the French President's residence. He breathed in the heady fragrance of the summer blooms and passed a fountain and the elaborate rear gates of the Élysée Palace. Perhaps he'd been too hasty with his dislike of Paris. He was enjoying the summer air, the fragrance, and light breeze. He also thought meeting Murray fortuitous even if he didn't warm to the man. But did he trust this man? *Trust*. His mind lingered over the word. There were so few in the world who could actually be trusted. He thought of the people he had on that list. His mother, Jenkins, he paused. In fact, he thought his maid, Dorothy, who he didn't really know, was perhaps more trustworthy than either of the people on his short list. Perhaps there wasn't anyone who fitted the description. Turning into Rue du Faubourg St Honoré, he walked towards the enormous front door of the British Embassy and rang the bell. A household official opened it.

'I'm here to meet with Mr Murray.'

'Is he expecting you, Sir?'

'Yes.'

'This way then, Sir,' the official said. Alistair walked across a stone paved inner courtyard and towards another elaborate but significantly smaller entry door. As he approached the steps, the door opened.

'It's alright Cummins. Come in Alistair.' Murray ushered Alistair across the marble tiled entry foyer and into an elaborately furnished sitting room on the ground floor at the rear. Alistair sank into the green leather chair with a view of the manicured garden beyond.

'It may interest you to know that I've arrange for Sir Richard to attend this evening's event at the Soviet Embassy.'

'So, what are you then?'

'Legal Advisor. Officially. But I report to Sir William Trant. I'm sure you've heard of him.'

'I know who the head of MI6 is.'

'Sir Richard will be able to answer all the necessary questions you may have. So why not leave it to him to find out about the scientist.'

'Who said I was interested in a scientist?'

'Come now! What other intention would you have for attempting to gain entry to the Soviet Embassy? I do know about Herr Friedleman.'

Alistair leaned back in the chair. 'I can't discuss that.'

Murray sat in a chair facing Alistair, the ingratiating smile returning. 'Very laudable, I'm sure, but as Sir Giles has personally given us both instructions, perhaps it would be best for us to join forces?'

Alistair eyed the suave man seated before him. If he was a diplomat, he was good at his job. But was that all Murray was? Mentioning the head of MI6 may have been a complete ruse. Or he could really be an MI6 Intelligence Officer. Either way, the comment had Alistair's attention. It was a risk. But he was sitting in the British Embassy, not a back-packers hovel. And Murray or his immediate superior in Paris, Sir Richard

Greaves evidently had the ear of *Big-Ears* at home. 'Very well. I was asked to make contact with Herr Friedleman.'

'Ah, yes. Everyone is eager to meet the East Berlin scientist.' Murray stood, then checking his watch, walked towards the bar at the end of the room. 'Whisky?'

Alistair stared at Murray. He wasn't sure how much Murray knew, but he was beginning to feel that the legal advisor knew a lot more than just the Defence of the Realm Act and the existence of the East German scientist. 'It seems I'm the perpetual patsy.'

Murray chuckled, then handed the whisky glass to Alistair. 'Not patsy. Just inexperienced. Or it could be that Sir Giles is testing you?'

'Until?'

Murray sat, twisting the whisky glass in his hand. 'You don't dispute you're being tested then?'

'Perhaps.'

'To answer your question - till Monday, perhaps.'

'Why Monday?'

'Oh, come, come! We both know Friedleman has an appointment with M. Lebec at the Louvre on Monday.'

'Doesn't he?' Alistair asked.

'Oh, yes. That's legit.'

'So, what isn't?'

Murray stood and reached for Alistair's empty glass then wandered towards the bar and poured two more whiskies before returning to his chair. He passed a glass to Alistair. 'Your good health!'

'Is my health in question?'

Murray smirked. 'Put it this way. Your presence here and involvement with Friedleman has the potential to cause major embarrassment to our government. You wouldn't want that, I'm sure. So! It would be better if you found some other entertainment for this evening.'

'And what do I tell Sir Giles?'

'That the Soviets kept Friedleman tucked up in the embassy, and you couldn't get near him. Five days was a tall order, after all. Why don't you just leave it to us here, after all, we have access to our friends in Boulevard Lannes, and you don't.' Murray downed the last of his whisky. 'You're in over your head, Quinn. Just have a good time in Paris and go home on Tuesday. There's a good chap. That way you're sure to remain healthy.' He paused. 'And, just to be on the safe side, come and check in with me and let me know where you are from time to time, so I won't worry about you.'

Alistair left the British Embassy and walked towards Place de la Madeleine. He needed to think, and his dingy hotel room with its brown water and low ceilings wasn't the place. He wandered towards the café bar in Place de la Madeleine and sat at an outside table. He ordered a coffee and watched the traffic pass, his mind on the smooth diplomat. Murray warning him off Friedleman had only served to heighten his interest in the scientist. Alistair stared at the passing evening crowd as he sat in the café contemplating how much Murray knew about Friedleman. But, Alistair sensed that the conversation wasn't just about warning him off contacting Friedleman. His gut told him, that while Murray knew a lot more than he did, Alistair believed Murray had been fishing for information. Or perhaps he just wanted to know how much Sir Giles knew about the scientist. Regardless, something didn't feel right, and Alastair was beginning to realise that Merick-Smith may be as much in the dark as he was. So, if that were the case, what was MI6 not telling Merrick-Smith? There was only one way to find out. He finished his coffee, then tossed some coins onto the plate and walked towards the designer shops on the Rue de Faubourg St Honoré where he intended to purchase a dinner suit.

CHAPTER EIGHT

Paris

Friday 19th July – Afternoon

In the bright afternoon sunshine, Grace Quinn, the former Director General of MI5, stepped from the taxi near the Petit Palace and walked towards the Alexandar III Bridge. Crossing the elaborate structure, she paused halfway and leaned on the balustrade to stare at the river below. Below her a sight-seeing barge filled with tourists passed under the bridge, its wake causing the murky waters of the Seine to swirl. Within minutes, a man approached from the opposite side and stood about ten feet away from her, but there was no eye contact. He leaned on the rail, his face turned towards the river.

Grace continued to watch him in her peripheral vision. After one minute, the man edged his way closer to where she stood.

She turned. 'You took your time. What have you been doing? Shopping?'

Jenkins ignored the slur. Truth be told, he was afraid of his former boss. 'The flight was delayed.'

'I told you to keep Alistair in England.'

'I thought I took orders from Sir Giles.'

'Don't be impertinent.'

Jenkins paused as a couple passed them on the bridge. 'I did try to do as you asked. Actually, I told him to stay in Britain. But Sir Giles wanted him for a job. And *I* can't override him.'

'The inference being that I can.'

Jenkins didn't answer. Experience had taught him not to respond. It only brought more sarcasm. He leaned over the balustrade and stared at the river again.

'He's here,' Grace said.

'Who? Sir Giles?'

'Don't be obtuse! No, Jenkins. Alistair. Without consolation, Sir Giles selected him to come to Paris and make contact with an East German scientist named Friedleman who is staying at the Soviet Embassy.'

'Who?'

Grace turned to face Jenkins. 'Are you deliberately trying to be dull-witted?'

'I thought you'd retired.'

'We never retire. You, of all people, should know that.'

'And he's here? Alistair, I mean.'

'Yes,' Grace said her annoyance barely disguised.

'May I ask how you know this?'

Grace stiffened. 'How I know is irrelevant. You were told to keep Alistair at home. And you failed. Now that he is here, you must keep him under surveillance. He's unpredictable.'

'You don't have to tell me that,' Jenkins muttered.

'If that were true, you wouldn't have failed.'

Jenkins paused. 'Sorry. What do you want me to do?'

'Mind Alistair. Keep him busy. I'm sure you know his likes and dislikes. He's staying at the Hotel Nice in Rue Vignon. And, keep him away from the Soviet Embassy. I don't care how you do it. And that, Jenkins is an order!'

Jenkins heard the threat. He wasn't sure she could give him orders. Despite his years of service, he wondered just how Grace Quinn always managed to make lesser mortals feel as though they were beneath contempt and totally incompetent, even if they were neither. 'How do I reach you, if I need to?'

She dropped a packet of cigarettes to the pavement then stamped on it. 'Telephone the number inside. I've rented a small apartment for you. It's on the left bank in Rue de la Huchette. Number 20, top floor. The key's in the packet too.'

'Thanks.'

'Don't get too excited.'

He watched her walk away, then bent to pick up the flattened packet of *Gitanes*. She had a way of walking that was both assertive and defiant. Yet while he watched her, she blended into the crowd and Jenkins couldn't see her anymore. He drew in a long breath and glanced over the edge at the river. Grace Quinn. He was both afraid and in awe of her. And the well-known adage of not suffering fools was invented for her, if not by her. He felt in his pocket for the squashed packet of cigarettes. As he crossed the bridge to the right bank, he withdrew the packet and flipped it open. On the lining paper he read the address, Rue de la Huchette, Number 20. Top floor. Left Bank. He pocketed the key then checked his watch, four o'clock. Alistair, Jenkins surmised, wouldn't be in his room at the hotel at four in the afternoon. Unless, of course, he wasn't alone. But, come dark, Jenkins believed Alistair would either be outside the Soviet Embassy attempting to con his way in, or in Paris's red-light district looking for evening entertainment. And Jenkins wasn't sure how he was going to stop Alistair engaging in either of those pursuits.

Jenkins walked on, cutting through the gardens, heading for Place de la Madeleine. In the north-east corner of the square, he saw a bar where he could sit outside at a small table on the pavement and only just around the corner from Rue Vignon. He thought it likely that Alistair would return to his hotel via the large square. But it wasn't the only route. He checked the square again, scrutinizing every face. Then he took the side street that intersected with Rue Vignon. He could see the hotel entrance not fifty yards away. Despite wanting a drink, he couldn't risk missing Alistair. He loitered at the intersection with Rue Vignon, but half an hour passed, and he hadn't sighted Alistair. Turning a full three hundred and sixty degrees, he decided to check with the concierge at the Hotel Nice. There was always the risk that the concierge would inform Alistair that someone was asking about him, and could describe him, but he couldn't waste any more time. Alistair had to be located. As Jenkins strode towards the hotel, he saw a taxi pull up not fifty yards in front of him. Alistair alighted. He was carrying a bag with an expensive designer's logo emblazoned on the outside. Jenkins watched him walk into the hotel. 'Cheeky bastard! MI5 better not be paying for that!' Jenkins muttered. But the purchase of expensive designer clothes meant only one thing. Jenkins's mind recalled how Alistair had played a hunch over another Soviet operative, Vasali Vlatkov, a KGB agent. That Russian was cooling his heels at Her Majesty's pleasure. And it had exposed a dangerous leak in Britain's Security Service at the time. That was then. On British soil. But now? On French soil? Alistair could wind up imprisoned on espionage charges by the French or dead from a Soviet assassin's bullet. Jenkins hurried along the pavement towards the hotel wondering if he should defy both his masters and make contact with Alistair. He didn't know the alias Alistair was using, and he didn't wish to arouse any suspicion with the hotel reception staff. He waited. Wandering along Rue Vignon, he stared into shop windows. One was a pharmacy, the faded pictures in the window were of Rubenesque babies being fed some slop. Others were for headache pills and Vaseline, the cure-all for every ailment or so the poster claimed. The next shop was a photographic studio. Just as he was beginning to wonder if he'd been wrong about Alistair's evening pursuits, he saw the hotel door open.

Alistair emerged all preened and dressed for the evening in a white dinner jacket and bow tie. Jenkins hurriedly turned to face the shop window. 'Bloody hell! You look like a gangster,'

Jenkins muttered to himself. He turned to see Alistair walking towards Place de la Madeleine. Jenkins followed, quickening his pace. From the corner he saw Alistair hail a taxi.

***

The telephone on Boyanski's desk rang. 'We need to meet.'

'Again?'

'This isn't routine, Boyanski.'

Boyanski felt the blood rush. The voice was that of his contact and calling directly meant only one thing; something was Most Urgent. 'When?'

'Now!'

'But the embassy is hosting a party this evening. I will be expected to be here. Can't you tell me over the phone?'

'This isn't a request! Usual place, ten minutes.'

Boyanski checked the time. He reached for the telephone receiver again and dialled the extension number for Goskova. She answered after only two rings.

'Irina, I have to go out for half an hour.'

'But Major Boyanski, the Ambassador will not be happy if you are not here.'

'It can't be helped. I won't be long, and you can keep him busy. If he asks, just say my dinner suit hasn't arrived from the cleaners and I'll join you as soon as I can.'

***

Jenkins ran towards the taxi as an older woman got out. Pushing past her, he got into the rear seat. She glared at him, muttering something about rude foreigners.

'Where to?' the driver asked.

'You see that cab up there stopped by the pedestrian crossing? Follow it! Not too close!'

'You English?'

'Yes. Does it matter?'

The taxi driver shrugged. 'It explains a lot. What is it with you English! It's always the cloaks and the daggers.'

'Just don't lose it.'

The cab turned right, heading away from the Madeleine church then headed first north then east. Jenkins kept his eyes on the vehicle, but instinct told him where Alistair was headed. At the Arc de Triomphe, the cab headed left again. Jenkins felt his mouth go dry. He knew Alistair would try something. Something that could get him killed, and he knew who Grace Quinn would blame for her wayward son's death. Dread churned in Jenkins's gut whenever he thought about the former Director General. Why was Grace Quinn even there in Paris? He felt as though he was caught between a cobra and a mongoose. And he wasn't sure which one was which. 'When the taxi pulls up, you do the same but keep a good distance from it. Understand?'

'Oui.'

Jenkins paid the fare and got out. He saw Alistair standing on the pavement opposite the intimidating concrete structure. Jenkins looked along the street then at the formidable building that was the Soviet Embassy. 'Bloody hell!' he whispered. Several cars were parked along Boulevard Lannes, and people wearing evening dress were gathering around the gate.

Jenkins stopped as Alistair looked up to cross the road. Alistair turned to face him, and their eyes met. Alistair waved. Jenkins felt his heart stop. The gesture not only connected them, but it would also have been recorded on the Soviet cameras trained on the street. 'What are you doing here? They won't let you in dressed like that!' Alistair shouted.

'Are you fucking mad! Or just plain stupid! Bravado is one thing. Stupidity quite another. You've compromised us both, you idiot!' Jenkins ran along the footpath and stood next to the bus stop, pretending to read the bus timetable on the pole. Then he stood back as though he didn't know Alistair. He hoped the Soviet camera monitors would think Alistair's wave had been to hail an approaching bus. But dressed as he was, it wasn't likely. Across the road, the gate into the Soviet Embassy opened. The waiting evening guests parted to allow a black car with darkened windows through. Two seconds later, the gates slammed shut. Jenkins stared after the car that had driven away at speed. 'Did you see who was inside?'

'No.'

The guest queue reformed. One guest, a tall man with greying hair and a commanding presence was staring at them from his place in the queue.

'Who's that?' Alistair asked Jenkins.

'I don't know. Could be one of ours. Regardless, I think we should leave.'

Alistair stepped off the pavement.

'Where are you going?' Jenkins asked.

'To join the queue.'

'The hell you are! I don't like the way that car drove away. Too fast. Something doesn't feel right. If there's something going on here, they'll check the surveillance cameras and see us. Whatever is going on, we don't want to be anywhere near here.'

'You worry too much Jenkins. By the way, why are you here?'

'To baby-sit you.'

'On whose orders?'

'Does it matter?'

Alistair shrugged. 'Whatever's going on, Murray will tell us.'

'Murray? Murray who?'

'Someone from the British Embassy.'

'How do you know him?'

'He warned me off coming this evening.'

'Well, that's confirmed it. Something is definitely going on, and our presence could compromise it.'

'That's essentially what Murray said.'

'Bloody hell, Alistair! And you came anyway? They'll throw the book at you. And me! You come with me now or I'll expose you as the danger you are. And you can kiss goodbye to your career with MI5! It's over,' Jenkins said, but he thought it probably also applied to him. His mouth was dry, and he needed a drink. The fear of losing his job was secondary to the wrath he expected to receive from the mongoose.

'Ok, keep your shirt on, Jenkins. I'll come. Maybe I can get my money back on the suit.'

'I think that will be the least of your troubles,' Jenkins added.

CHAPTER NINE

Paris

Friday 19th July – Early Evening

Ivkin stood beside his bedroom window on the third floor of the Soviet Embassy, his gaze on the growing activity in the street below. The afternoon light was already fading, and a balmy evening was enveloping the city in its subtle allure. But twilights were long, and it wouldn't be dark for some hours. He scanned the faces gathering at the gate, his eye lingering on a tall man standing on the pavement opposite. He was young with loose curly dark hair and wore a white evening jacket. Although it appeared he was waiting for the next bus, Ivkin could see that he was staring at the building. Then quite suddenly he waved to someone further along the street that Ivkin couldn't yet see. When finally a man did come into view,

Ivkin could see that this man was not wearing evening attire. And, it appeared that he was either flustered at perhaps missing his bus or the two men knew each other. Ivkin continued to watch. They spoke briefly, but there was no cordiality between them . In fact, Ivkin believed there was some animosity. They exchanged a few words, then stood apart by the bus stop. Ivkin frowned. Despite their attempts to distance themselves from each other, Ivkin believed they were not strangers waiting for the next bus. The presence of these two men outside the Soviet Embassy troubled him. Below him, he saw one of the embassy cars drive away. With such an important function on this evening, he knew it would not have been the ambassador. He made a mental note to ask Boyanski about it. He checked his watch. He needed to dress.

Boyanski, or more likely Irina Goskova, had found a dinner suit for him to wear and had left it hanging on the wardrobe. Ivkin tried it on, his mind still on the two men outside. While he understood the West's surveillance of the Soviet Embassy would be routine, Friedleman's arrival in Paris had evidently sent the West into a flurry of conspicuous activity. He found himself smiling; he believed the Americans at the checkpoint in Berlin had wasted no time in passing on this information. A knock on his door broke his concentration. Pulling his jacket on, he opened the door. Goskova stood in the hall.

'Colonel Ivkin. You are not wearing your medals?'

'You may recall Comrade Goskova, I didn't know I'd be in Paris, so my medals are at home.'

'Of course.' Goskova hovered.

'Is there something I can help you with?' Ivkin asked, seeing the woman still standing in his doorway.

'I would just like to inform you that Major Boyanski asked me to provide him with details of your career. He would like to ask you about your time in the Far East. And your role in spying on the British in Hong Kong.'

'And what did you find out?'

'Not much.'

Ivkin nodded. 'Perhaps it would be best if Major Boyanski asked me himself. Is he already downstairs?'

'No. He went out. I don't know where. He said he wouldn't be long.'

'I see.' Ivkin paused. 'Miss Goskova, do you know why Major Boyanski asked you to research my early career?'

'I don't think he meant any offence, Colonel Ivkin. I think he is a little in awe of you, if I'm honest about it.'

'Honesty is a wise practice when speaking with superior officers. You never know who is listening.'

Goskova smiled. 'Do you have everything you need, Colonel?'

'For now. But perhaps I can save you some time with your research endeavours. You can inform Major Boyanski that as a colonel in the KGB, it would be most unwise to have pictures of myself printed in any publications. There can be no information, pictorial or written about me available in Western publications or indeed anywhere outside the Soviet Union.' Ivkin paused. 'If I thought that Major Boyanski was inquiring about me for any other reason, I would have to inform Moscow Central Committee of this. Perhaps Boyanski has been too long in the West. Perhaps there are too many temptations here for him in Paris. I wonder if he should be removed to one of our lesser embassies in the third world or a posting in Vladivostok.'

'I will inform him of your concerns on his return. But I'm sure he meant no disrespect. In fact, I believe he wants to learn as much as he can from you while you are in Paris, Colonel.'

'Then we'll say no more about it. We should go down. The guests are arriving.'

'Of course, Colonel Ivkin.'

They walked along the corridor stopping outside Friedleman's room. Ivkin knocked on the door.

A few seconds later Friedleman opened his door and stepped into the corridor. 'Grigori, do I look alright?'

'You look fine, Kurt. Unlike me, your suit is your own, and it fits you.'

'I'm so grateful you're here with me.'

Ivkin ushered Friedleman along the corridor, leaving Goskova standing in the hall. 'Enjoy yourself tonight, Kurt,' Ivkin said as they stepped into the lift. 'There'll be French dignitaries to meet and other foreign diplomats. Stick to your expert subject. They will be impressed. I understand Monsieur Lebec will be attending.'

'Oh, that's wonderful! It's all a bit overwhelming. I'm so glad you're here.'

Stepping from the lift into the front entry foyer, they saw a line of well-dressed people assembling at the entrance. Two security guards stood on either side of the front hall. A further official stood beside the door into the large reception room, introducing each guest by name as they queued to meet the Ambassador and his wife. A minute later he saw Boyanski and Goskova walk past them, both going to stand to one side of the official party. Ivkin studied Boyanski. He thought

Boyanski looked flustered, as though he'd dressed in a hurry. He knew Goskova had informed him that Boyanski had gone out, and he wondered where Boyanski had gone. And whom he'd met. Evidently Boyanski thought it important enough to leave the embassy at short notice but whatever had taken him away hadn't lasted long. Surely that could only be to share information. Information that couldn't be shared by telephone from the embassy. He decided for now, to keep Boyanski's hurried trip away from the embassy to himself. Compromising intelligence was always useful and wasted if disclosed too early. Ivkin led Friedleman inside and took two glasses of champagne from a tray. 'After the guests have met the ambassador, I'll introduce you to him and his wife and then to M. Lebec.'

'How do I address these people?' Kurt whispered.

'By name, Kurt. But a word of advice; just keep your conversation to art and sculpture.' Ivkin's eyes scanned the growing crowd in the room. Near the entry door, he saw Irina Goskova moving adroitly among the guests.

'I need to check something. I'll be back in a minute.'

Friedleman's eyes widened. 'Where are you going?'

'You'll be fine, Kurt. You need not be so nervous. Just keep to your subjects and everything will be alright.'

Ivkin walked towards Boyanski and stood beside him. 'A word, Boyanski.'

'Can it wait?'

'No. Do you have the guest list for this evening's event?'

'Yes. Why do you ask?'

'Where is it?'

'In my office. And there's a copy at the entry.'

'Your office is best.'

'As you wish.' Boyanski led Ivkin along a winding corridor to the rear of the building and entered a four-digit code into the door lock. 'Something worrying you, Colonel Ivkin? Do you suspect something, comrade colonel?'

'It's a hunch at present, Boyanski. I just want to see the guest list.'

Boyanski unlocked the first of three filing cabinets then took a file from the second drawer and placed it on his desk. Ivkin leaned over the document, his gaze scanning the names. He pointed to one. 'Sir Richard Greaves. He's from the British Embassy. Is he here yet? Why was he invited?'

'He is the Cultural Attaché at the British Embassy.'

'Are other Cultural Attachés invited, those from other embassies?'

'I'll check. What do you suspect?'

'I suspect everyone until proven otherwise, Boyanski. And no, I'll check. You stay with Friedleman. It must be expected that the British and the Americans would want Friedleman. So, we must be alert to anything unusual. Do you have anything to report to me, Boyanski?'

'No. But you asked about Sir Richard. He was a last minute invited guest,' Boyanski added.

'Really?' Ivkin paused. 'So we must assume that no other Cultural Attachés have been invited. I want to know why he was included. You know, Boyanski that many Cultural Attachés are not employed for cultural reasons.'

'I am aware of their other duties for their various countries.'

'So, if he has been invited, then we must be more than vigilant. Who invited this Sir Richard Greaves?'

'It was a request from the British Embassy.'

'Really. And you normally acquiesce to British Embassy requests?'

'Of course not, Colonel Ivkin. But I saw no harm in it. This evening is a formal event for the Swedish Ambassador, and there are a large number of people attending. Our security guards are on high alert.'

Ivkin kept his steady gaze on Boyanski. He noted that Boyanski hadn't informed him why he'd left the embassy so hurriedly. Or if anyone other than the driver was with him. But when the time was right, when Boyanski felt vulnerable, Ivkin would question him about his brief absence. Always best done when a target feels most vulnerable. It usually led to a vomit of information designed to establish innocence. 'I have to inform you, Boyanski; there was a man standing outside the embassy this afternoon. A man I recognise. He works for British Intelligence. Watch Friedleman closely. If Greaves is already inside, we must get Friedleman away. The British couldn't know what Friedleman looks like, but it will take Greaves only minutes to put a face to the name.' Ivkin turned to leave. 'Hurry, Boyanski. Don't leave Friedleman alone for a second.' Boyanski ran out of his office and down the corridor, his heavy shoes pounding on the polished floors. With Boyanski gone, Ivkin quickly checked all the drawers and cupboards in the KGB major's office. Inside one, he saw two coats, several hats and a bullet-proof vest. Ivkin closed the cupboard then returned the file to the cabinet. Opening the lower filing cabinet drawer, he saw a pistol. A military issued Makarov PM in its brown leather pouch. Beside it was a box of ammunition. Ivkin grabbed the pouch and the rounds and pushed them into his trouser pocket, the ill-fitting jacket hiding the weapon.

Closing the door to Boyanski's office, Ivkin hurried to the front door where he stood behind the guard checking off the guests as they arrived. He saw the name. Returning to the large reception room he rejoined Boyanski. 'He's here. We don't want a scene. And it mustn't look like we suspect anything. I'll get Friedleman out. Is there a car I can use? I'll take him to a KGB safe-house and call you once we're there. And Boyanski get his suitcase from his room. We may need to be in the safe house a few days.'

'Of course, Colonel Ivkin. I'll have Comrade Goskova collect his belongings and arrange the car now. There's a safe house in Rue Rollin, near the Pantheon. Sergei, the driver knows where it is. But be careful. It is close to the Sorbonne. The students are still protesting, and there were riots there in May. I'll call the housekeeper to expect you. You should leave by the side door.'

'Once we are away, stay with Greaves. When he leaves the embassy, have one of your people follow him!'

Ivkin returned to the reception room. He could see Friedleman standing beside Monsieur Lebec. He edged towards them. 'Monsieur Lebec. I am Grigori Ivkin. It is an honour to meet you, and we are very excited about seeing you on Monday. Kurt, can I have a word? Please excuse us, M. Lebec.'

'Grigori, what is it?'

'We must hurry. I need to get you out. Your life is in danger,' Ivkin whispered. 'A known British assassin has gained entry. We must leave now. We have a safe-house in Paris where I will take you. Just move slowly and don't say anything. If anyone asks, you're going to the toilet.'

Ivkin ushered Friedleman along the corridor and out the side entrance to where a car with darkened windows stood waiting.

'Grigori, what's happening?'

'It will be alright, Kurt. Just stay calm. I have everything under control. Now just get in and lie low on the rear seat. Just in case.'

The car drove through the gates and past the late arriving guests then sped across Paris to the Left Bank. Ivkin leaned forward and called to the driver. 'Do not drop us off anywhere near the Sorbonne or the safe house. If we are being followed, I need it to remain safe. We'll get out near the Luxembourg Gardens and walk the rest of the way.'

The driver pulled up by the tall iron railings of the Luxembourg Palace, and Ivkin and Friedleman got out. Ivkin scanned the streets and buildings around them. People were everywhere. Some appeared to be out enjoying the evening, others were with children, others coming and going from the palace gardens. Only a few were students. Ivkin checked them all, watching their behaviour. But none were simply watching. He glanced at Friedleman. He could see the tension on his face and by the way he grasped his suitcase. 'We'll enter the gardens here, Kurt. If we stand by the pond, I can check the surrounding area for anyone watching us. Then we'll leave via the far side of the palace.' They wandered along the gravel paths beside the flower beds that led to the pond. Nearby, children were sailing toy boats on the water. People came and went, the remaining students were sitting in groups, some still with placards. 'Are we safe here, Grigori?' Friedleman asked.

'Crowds are good, Kurt. We'll mingle among them. Anyone watching us will soon lose sight of us here.'

'Is someone trying to kill me?' Friedleman whispered.

'Not kill, Kurt. Kidnap, possibly. I didn't want the driver to take us directly to the safe house. If anyone was following us, the car would have led them to our safe-house and to you.'

'I'm so glad you're here. I wouldn't know what to do.'

'Just come with me and you'll be alright.'

***

Boyanski strode into the reception room, his eye searching for Irina. Seeing her talking to some guests, he slowly approached the group and taking her by the elbow, led her away from the gathering crowd. 'Irina, come with me.'

'Major? Is something wrong? I did as you asked. I arranged the car and packed Herr Friedleman's suitcase, as you instructed.'

'Not here. My office.'

Boyanski unlocked his office door then closed it behind them. 'Irina, there is an Englishman here, Sir Richard Greaves. Do you know what he looks like?'

'Yes. He was talking with the Monsieur Lebec and Herr Friedleman. He's the Cultural Attaché at the British Embassy.'

'That's his official title. But most likely he's MI6. As soon as he leaves us, you are to follow him. I want to know where Sir Richard goes when he leaves here. As soon as Greaves returns to the British embassy, telephone me.'

'I noticed Colonel Ivkin escort Herr Friedleman from the reception room. As you asked me to get Herr Friedleman's suitcase, I can only guess that they have left the embassy?'

'Yes. But tell no one.'

'Is something wrong?'

'Perhaps. Best Herr Friedleman isn't here. Now you should return to the party. As soon as Greaves leaves, follow him.'

'Should I take Sergei?'

'He's taking Colonel Ivkin and Herr Friedleman to a safe house. He won't be gone more than an hour. I'll let you know once he's back. If Greaves tries to leave before Sergei returns, keep him busy here. Then follow him. But tell Sergei not to use the official embassy car. Greaves mustn't know he's being followed.'

'Sir.'

Goskova left to find Sir Richard. He was standing in a group talking with Monsieur Lebec. Irina took a glass of champagne from the tray and wandered towards the curator.

'I trust you are enjoying yourself, Monsieur Lebec, Sir Richard.'

Greaves smiled. 'I understand you are to meet with Herr Friedleman on Monday, Monsieur?'

'Oui. I am looking forward to that very much. I admire the work of this sculptor.'

Greaves turned to Irina. 'Where is he? I noticed he left the room. I hope you haven't whisked him away?'

'Like us all, Sir Richard, he must attend to the call of nature. Monsieur Lebec, I would very much like to show you our art collection. We have a collection much envied by the West. And currently we have painting on loan from our State Hermitage

Museum. A Leonardo da Vinci, The Madonna and Child, painted by Da Vinci between 1480 and 1490. In fact it is one of two Leonard de Vinci paintings in the State Hermitage collection.'

'I'd very much like to see that.'

Irina took Lebec's elbow and escorted him across the room to where the famous painting hung, leaving Greaves standing alone.

From the corner of her eye, she watched Greaves. He drained his drink then reached for another from a passing waiter. Leaving Lebec drooling over the Leonardo Da Vinci, she rejoined Greaves.

'Very clever, Miss Goskova.'

'Please allow me to introduce you to our ambassador.'

'We've met.'

'Then, perhaps our other French guests.'

Greaves leaned in and whispered. 'I will play your game, but you can't keep him locked up forever.'

Half an hour later, Boyanski appeared in the doorway, and Irina knew that Sergei had returned. She was pleased. Keeping the Englishman occupied had been harder than she'd appreciated.

Making her excuses, she went to the garage to find Sergei. He was in the driver's office chatting with Ivan, the mechanic. Both men stood as soon as Irina poked her head around the door. 'Sergei, we have to follow someone tonight. Get an unofficial car and park at the side entrance. I'll join you there.'

'Where's the target currently?'

'He's one of the guests here. He could leave at any time, so you must be ready to go at a moment's notice. I must get back to the reception, in case he leaves soon.'

Sergei sat again.

'Now, Sergei. As soon as I come to the side door, we need to leave.'

Sergei nodded. 'Ok. I'll be there in five minutes.'

Goskova returned upstairs and met Boyanski in the hall. 'Greaves is leaving,' Boyanski told her. 'Says he feels unwell. Don't lose sight of him, Irina. And, here, take this,' Boyanski said, thrusting a small camera into her hands. 'Photograph anyone he meets.'

Goskova hurried to her small office adjacent to Boyanski's and hung her green cape on the stand in the corner, replacing it with a long cream macintosh coat. She shoved the camera into her pocket. Moving quickly, she left the embassy by the side door and walked straight to the car and sat in the rear seat.

Keeping her eyes glued to the main gate she saw the British Cultural Attaché leave. 'That's him,' she whispered. Sergei started the engine and allowed the car to inch forward. She could see Greaves walk through the gate, then towards a black *Jaguar* car parked a little further down the street. The Soviet Embassy gate opened. Sergei waited to allow the traffic to pass. Down the street, Goskova saw Greaves get into his car.

'Don't lose him, Sergei,' she said.

***

Greaves stormed into the small reception room on the ground floor of the British Embassy where Murray had put Alistair and Jenkins. Greaves was still dressed in his evening attire. Jenkins stood as Greaves approached as though the Queen had just entered the room. Alistair remained seated.

'Murray tells me you are the person Sir Giles sent to Paris?'

Alistair stood. 'I am.'

'Well! Would you care to explain your actions?'

'How do you do? Sir Richard Greaves, I presume?' Alistair said calmly extending his hand.

'That's enough of your impertinence! You were told to stay away from the Soviet Embassy. But you went anyway. And you were seen. And not just by me! You were specifically told by Murray not to go to the Soviet Embassy! And by your incompetence and flagrant disregard for instructions, you have single-handedly made any attempt to meet Friedleman well-nigh impossible. He was whisked away from this evening's function, and we have you to thank for that! You have endangered not only lives but valuable assets. The Soviet security guards were on high alert for anyone trying to gain unauthorized entry. Your stunt was not only foolish, but it was also amateurish in the extreme. They were meant to send an unknown not an incompetent.' His steely gaze shifted to Jenkins. 'And who are you?'

'Jenkins, Sir. MI5.'

'Jenkins. You should know better. As I understand it, you were also told to keep him away from the Soviet Embassy. You'll both collect your belongings, move in here and take the first flight home tomorrow. You've done enough damage for one night.'

'May I ask how you knew I was there, Sir Richard?' Alistair asked.

'I saw you. Outside. Dressed in your Hollywood attire. You stood out! Never a good thing in our line of work. And, Murray told me about meeting you this afternoon outside the Soviet Embassy. Why Sir Giles picked you to come is beyond belief.'

Alistair stared at the irate Cultural Attaché. He had so many questions arising from what Sir Richard had just said, but he knew Greaves wouldn't be in any mood to answer them. 'And now we have another problem. Friedleman left the reception in somewhat of a hurry. If Friedleman has been removed from the embassy, we have no idea where they're taken him. For all we know, he may not even be in Paris now.'

'Perhaps I can be of service after all. I will find Herr Friedleman,' Alistair said.

The door opened, and Murray joined the group. 'So you went anyway.'

'You informed Sir Richard?' Alistair asked.

'Of course. We have no secrets.'

'Mr Quinn here says he will find wherever they've hidden Herr Friedleman,' Greaves said.

'I think that highly unlikely,' Murray added. He settled himself into a chair by the window, his gaze fixed on Alistair.

Alistair kept his eye on Murray. He was beginning to feel that Murray had taken a personal dislike to him. Although he didn't know why. Regardless, the feeling was mutual. 'You want the East German scientist. And that car that sped away from the Embassy; what's the chance that it was bundling Herr

Friedleman away to a safe house somewhere in Paris. I'll find him.'

Jenkins stared at Alistair. 'And how will you do that?'

'We're waiting?' Greaves added, his eyes fixed on Alistair.

Alistair grinned. He felt confident he knew where he'd get the information he needed, but he wasn't going to tell either Jenkins or Greaves. And he needed to get Jenkins off his back. He stared at Greaves, then Murray. Not too suave now, he thought, hoping he held the upper hand. But they had to be told something. All his schoolboy years of conjuring quick but plausible alibis now proved their worth. 'We know he's got an appointment on Monday at the Louvre at ten. So, the Soviets will hide him until then. He'll also have a minder or two with him. My guess is that this safe house will be in a high foot traffic area, like near a hospital or university. And given what happened in May, the area around the Sorbonne will have loads of angry students. Lots of people coming and going.' Alistair paused waiting for a reaction from any of the three men in the room. No one spoke.

'Well? Is that it? That's your plan! To knock on several thousand doors amongst enormous crowds of people in the hope of finding him?' Murray said.

Alistair scanned their faces. He knew by their expressions that what motivated Greaves's and Jenkins's silence couldn't have been more different. Jenkins, Alistair believed, hadn't spoken because he didn't know what to say. Greaves, on the other hand, did what all diplomats do when a solution is required, wait for others to speak. But Murray's outburst and expression was a mix of intimidatory sarcasm, cynicism and skepticism. Alistair smiled. 'I've got two days to locate him. Then, when I do, I disappear, and you can snatch him whenever you want.'

CHAPTER TEN

Paris

Friday 19th July – Late Evening

Grace Quinn sat by the open French doors of her first floor apartment in Rue Ste-Croix de la Bretonnerie, a glass of gin and tonic in her hand. She took a sip, then twisted the glass in her hand, her eye on the evening sky, her mind on the job ahead. It had become complicated in a way she'd not anticipated. That wasn't right. She always expected the unexpected. But this unexpected had the potential to derail the entire mission; a plan that had taken years to set up just waiting for the right moment to unleash. The telephone on the table beside her rang.

She picked up the telephone receiver. 'Yes?'

'Bill here, Grace.'

She waited.

'He tried to get in, just as you thought he would.'

'And Jenkins?'

'According to Greaves, Alistair compromised him. I can't get Alistair out if he's under orders from Giles. But you can get Jenkins out of Paris at least. He's no use now.'

There was silence for a few seconds before Grace spoke again. 'I'll keep Jenkins busy, but I want him here.'

'Your reason?'

'Always useful to have someone on standby. And Bill. Get a backup team into Paris.'

'You foresee problems?'

'Always.'

'I'm glad you're on our side, Grace.'

Grace replaced the telephone receiver, then drained the drink. Rising, she poured herself another gin and tonic then returned to the chair by the open French doors, her gaze on the architectural beauty of the building opposite in the soft, evening light. She thought of all the people involved. There was always the possibility of something unplanned occurring. Indeed, in such a complicated deception, something will go wrong. That was to be expected. But with a back-up team in place, any overt unforeseen consequences could, at least, be controlled. And, despite Alistair's arrival in Paris, the deception could still work just so long as information was forthcoming. And Merrick-Smith stayed out of it. She pursed her lips as she thought about Giles Merrick-Smith. She'd never been in favour of his elevation to the top job, but unlike Giles, she'd never found manipulating people difficult. And, she surmised Alistair had inherited the same useful trait. She understood how Philby had been so successful at evading suspicion. Manipulation and outrageous lies kept honest people in the dark. And not-so-honest people were bought. You just had to know them. How they thought and what motivated them, and all their foibles and vices. Then their reactions could be predicted. Jenkins was easy. Loyal and predictable even to a fool. A by-the-book sort of operative best kept at home. Alistair was another matter entirely. She smirked, then raised the glass to her lips. 'But don't think for one minute, my son that you can outwit me!'

The telephone on her desk rang again. Placing the glass on the small table she picked up the receiver.

'Ma'am, it's Jenkins.'

An audible sigh flowed into the telephone receiver. 'I didn't think it was Father Christmas. Well?'

'Alistair compromised me, so he knows I'm here and why.'

'And?'

'And, according to Sir Richard Greaves, the East German scientist was whisked away from the Soviet Embassy during the evening. Most likely to a safe house in Paris. Alistair says he's going to try to locate Friedleman. He says he'll find him over the weekend.'

'Where are you calling from?'

'Our embassy. Sir Richard Greaves and a man called Murray, the Legal Advisor here at the embassy said Alistair and I can stay here. But Greaves wants us to fly home tomorrow. I'll go with Alistair to the hotel to collect his things.'

'No! You're both to stay in Paris. But neither of you are to stay in the embassy. We cannot have any connection between our diplomatic staff and Alistair. He's a loose cannon and could do anything. Take him to the flat I rented for you. And Jenkins,'

'Ma'am?'

'Not a word to anyone about where you'll be. No one, I repeat, no one, not even the Prime Minister is to know where you'll be, do you hear me? And don't let Alistair out of your sight.'

***

Ivkin led Friedleman along the tree lined avenue of the Luxembourg Palace then towards the side gate into Rue de Vaugirard. Circling behind the Luxembourg Palace, he took Friedleman into a narrow street where rundown four storey buildings housed medical students from the Sorbonne and mediocre artists of all nationalities. Evening had descended, and the narrow passageways of the Latin Quarter were already in shadow, the only light coming from the many bars and restaurants. Everywhere was crowded with opinionated students discussing social reform, rock music or the world's uncertain future, their voices audible in the street. Stopping by a recessed doorway on the right, Ivkin led Friedleman up a dilapidated flight of stairs that had seen only scant repairs and unlocked the door. 'It's a bit squalid. Sorry. It probably hasn't been in use for a while.'

Friedleman sat on an old, dusty velvet covered chair near the window. 'What's going on, Grigori?'

'I believe the British are trying to snatch you, Kurt. We have to stay one step ahead.'

'Is this our safe house?'

'I know it doesn't look attractive, but it's functional and out of the way. It will serve our purposes.' Ivkin sat on a wooden chair by a table. 'I have no wish to alarm you, but this afternoon, I saw a tall man standing outside the embassy. And, I don't believe he was waiting for the bus. He was joined by a man I recognise as a British Intelligence Officer. Also, the Cultural Attaché from the British Embassy was a last-minute invited guest at this evening's soirée. And Cultural Attaché is usually another word for spy. It's almost certain they are planning something. If we stay low, we'll make the appointment on Monday, then we can leave the West. The Louvre is not too far away. We won't be seen here. I'll check on everything and make sure a car from our embassy collects us on Monday and takes us to the airport that afternoon.'

'Why do they want me?'

'They must know about you. Your work. Someone has passed on this information. Think, Kurt. Someone at your work, perhaps?' Ivkin paused. 'Is it possible Marlis could have told someone?'

'My God! Poor Marlis. But even if she did, she couldn't tell them anything. She's not a scientist. She wouldn't understand it.'

Ivkin leaned forward and held Friedleman's gaze. 'Could she have taken the notebook?'

Friedleman hung his head in his hands, then rubbed his face. 'I hope not!' he said then sobbed but only for a second before pulling himself together. 'I'm sorry, Grigori. I feel so…unsafe, I suppose. I don't know where I am or what to think. Without you, I would be totally at their mercy.'

Ivkin stood. 'I'll check the neighbourhood. And find us some food.' Ivkin paused. 'It's alright, Kurt. You are safe with me, I promise.'

'What should I do?'

'Lock the door after I leave. And don't let anyone in or leave here for any reason.'

Ivkin smiled, then opened the door and peered out. Stepping onto the landing, he closed the door behind him. He heard Friedleman lock the door from the inside. Descending the stairs, he stepped into the street. A few streets away he found a shop where he could buy some food. He guessed he had less than thirty minutes.

CHAPTER ELEVEN

Paris

Fri 19th July – Late Evening

Irina Goskova leaned forward in the seat her eyes fixed on the British Cultural Attaché's car as it pulled up at the rear gates into the British Embassy. It waited only moments before the gates opened, and the car disappeared inside. She wasn't sure why Major Boyanski had asked her to follow Sir Richard Greaves, but she wasn't going to ask. Boyanski had a temper, and she liked Paris. Although she felt sure it had something to do with the sudden departure of Colonel Ivkin and the East German scientist.

'Pull up here, Sergei,' she said. Thirty minutes passed, and the car had not reemerged. 'I should telephone Major Boyanski. There's a phone in a bar in Place de la Madeleine I know of. I won't be long. And watch to see if that car or any car comes out again.'

'If one does, do I follow it or wait for you?'

'Good question.' Irina thought. 'Follow it. I'll make my own way back, if you've gone from here when I return. And Sergei, don't lose it. Take this,' she said pulling the miniature camera from her coat pocket. 'If he meets anyone, take a photograph.' Goskova walked to the corner. As she turned into Rue Faubourg St Honoré, she glanced back. Even though twilight was declining, she could see Sergei sitting behind the wheel. She also saw the newspaper spread over the steering wheel. She strode towards Place de la Madeleine. Despite the hour, cars still swirled around the monumental church. But then, this was Paris, not East Berlin, and Paris at night was when Parisiens and the well-heeled came out to dine, drink wine and attend the Lido or Moulin Rouge. Hurrying, she crossed the square heading for the bar in the far corner. Opening the door, she stepped inside. The barman was behind the counter. His dark eyes looked up as she entered.

'Can I use the telephone?' she asked in French.

The barman nodded, indicating the rear of the salon with a tilt of his bald head. Goskova walked straight towards the small, recessed cubicle, then lifted the telephone receiver and reaching into her coat pocket, inserted the coins. She dialled the memorised number.

***

Alistair locked his small suitcase and closing the door on his tiny room, descended the stairs.

'I've paid the bill,' Jenkins said as Alistair joined him in the tiny lobby.

'I need a drink. There's a bar along the road,' Alistair said. He saw Jenkins skeptical expression. 'Surely one drink can't hurt?'

'Alright, but then it's a taxi. I don't want any more trouble.'

'Really Jenkins? You're beginning to sound like an old man. Maybe you should look for another line of employment.'

'Shut up!' Jenkins said, but he thought he may have to if anything else went pear-shaped and the mongoose learned about it. He didn't know how she did it, but she could reduce a subordinate to quivering jelly with just a look.

They walked in single file along the narrow footpath weaving between the parked cars and motorcycles on the footpath in Rue Vignon. Turning the corner into Place de la Madeleine, Alistair saw the red awnings ahead. He quickened his pace then opened the glass door to the bar. He counted the number of patrons and who was sitting where, as he entered;

his training and the habit of a lifetime for those employed in Her Majesty's Secret Service. He'd expected more people to be there, however, it was still too early for the post evening entertainment crowd to arrive. Standing at the counter, Alistair ordered two whiskies just as a stunningly good-looking young woman he recognised walked towards the bar. Her musky perfume filled the air as she approached. She was wearing a long trench coat over evening clothes and stiletto heels. An outfit not designed for a quick getaway. For a fleeting moment, he wondered why she was no longer at the Ambassador's cocktail party at the Soviet Embassy. By her dress and shoes, she'd evidently left in a hurry. He found himself smiling. In all of Paris, Irina Goskova was now beside him. And, there could only be one reason for her to be absent from the Soviet Embassy this night. His hunch about the car that had sped away from the embassy had, he felt sure, removed the East German scientist well away from some perceived threat. He wondered about that. But only for a second. Regardless, he thanked God for the sudden turn of events.

'Could I have a vodka?' she asked settling on a bar stool.

'Allow me,' Alistair said, placing several notes on the counter. The barman took the money and disappeared to pour the drinks.

'No. Thank you. It's fine, I can pay for myself.'

Alistair watched her. She was doing her best to disguise the thick foreign accent. 'Too late. Besides, I've never known a beautiful woman to refuse a drink from a gentleman?' Alistair pulled the packet of cigarettes from his coat pocket. He held the open packet towards the woman, and she withdrew one. He lit it for her. 'But I think you aren't French?' he said in Russian. He watched her closely.

For one second, her eyes flared. Then she drew back on the cigarette. 'What makes you say that?' she said in French.

'Just a hunch,' he said reaching for her hand and pulling it to his lips.

Jenkins joined him at the bar. 'Excuse us, Mademoiselle. Simon, we have to go. Simon!'

He'd almost forgotten his alias. 'I apologise for my friend's rudeness.' Alistair stood, then leaned in towards her, occupying her personal space. 'So, now you know my name, may I know yours?'

'Olga.'

'One moment, Olga, please.' Alistair turned to Jenkins. 'You go, I'll meet you there.'

'Not a chance.'

Alistair slid from the bar stool and stood with his back to the woman. 'Jenkins, this woman works for the Soviet Embassy,' he whispered. 'Take my suitcase and I'll meet you at the flat.'

'How do you know that?'

'Merrick-Smith gave me a photograph of her.'

'Bloody hell! Alistair, I was ordered not to leave you alone for a second.'

'If you think for one minute, I will allow you to stand at the foot of our bed, you have another think coming. Besides, I want her to tell me where Friedleman is, not scare her half to death.'

Jenkins chewed on his lower lip. 'I know I'm going to regret this. Ok. When you've finished,' he paused, 'questioning Miss whatever-her-name is, come to 20 Rue de la Huchette. Top floor. It's on the Left Bank off Place St Michel. The mon...err, your mother will most likely kill me. One hour. That's all. And don't disappear. Or there'll be hell to pay.'

Alistair smiled, then rejoined Irina.

'I have a car waiting for me outside. I must go,' she said.

'Supposing I say I know your name.'

'I just told you that.'

'No, you didn't, Irina.'

Her face fell. A tense silence ensued before she spoke. 'Who are you?'

'Someone who has fallen madly in love with you.' He leaned in close, his lips hovering over hers, the musk fragrance of her perfume filling his head. 'And I can get you to the West where you can buy shoes in every colour of the rainbow. And no one will ask you how much they cost nor where you bought them.'

She pulled back. A broad grin spread across her face. 'Confident, aren't you!'

'I'm hopelessly drawn to beautiful women. At least you'll have that drink with me?'

'Perhaps I will. But you haven't told me who you are?'

'You don't expect me to answer that, surely.' Alistair nodded to the barman. 'Two whiskies, please.'

Irina slipped off the stool. 'I have to powder my nose.'

'Don't be long,' Alistair said. He reached for her hand and kissed it. He watched her walk away, the alluring fragrance of her perfume lingering. He beckoned the barman over. 'You have a parcel for me, I think. Simon Cordery.'

The barman nodded, his gaze remaining on Alistair.

Alistair put a US fifty dollar note on the counter. A minute later, the barman handed him a small box wrapped in brown paper. Checking over his shoulder to see if anyone was watching him, he unwrapped the box, slid the L9A1 pistol into his coat pocket along with a small box of ammunition then handed the barman the empty box. Another US fifty was under the string.

'Is there a back way out of here?' Alistair asked.

The barman nodded.

Alistair hurried into the rear corridor and found the door to the back alley open. He ran to the end of the lane and looked in both directions. Running back into the bar to the front door, he hurried into the square. Peering over the heads of a growing crowd, he saw her hurrying towards Rue Royale.

He returned to the bar. 'Do you know her?' he asked the barman.

'She comes in here sometimes. Not often. But I can tell you this. That phone in back, it only makes local calls.'

Alistair smiled. 'Does she ever meet anyone?'

'Not that I recall. She uses the telephone. She is beautiful, n'est pas? But perhaps not for you,' the barman chortled.

'What's your name, in case I need something else?'

'Jean.'

Alistair smiled and left. He didn't believe the man's name was *Jean,* but it didn't matter. People like Jean never ceased to amaze him; they would sell their own mothers for money.

'Thank heaven for the corrupt,' he muttered as he ran. Darting between the speeding cars and dodging the blaring horns and angry fists of the incensed drivers, he crossed the crowded square and ran at full pace along Rue de Surène then turned into Rue d'Anjou hoping the shortcut would put him in front of her. As he turned into Rue Faubourg St Honoré, he saw her hurrying past the British Embassy. He moved quickly along the footpath on the opposite side of the street and crossed just before she turned into Rue de l'Élysée.

He reached for her waist and turned her quickly. 'I won't take your sudden departure as an insult. But I will be offended if you do not allow me to escort you back to the bar so we can finish our drinks. And, by the way, this isn't a safe place for you to be.'

Goskova glanced along the street to where she'd left Sergei sitting in the Soviet car. He was no longer there. She turned back and looked up at Alistair. 'Very well. But tell me now who you work for, or I will make a scene sufficient for the British Embassy cameras to see us.'

'Allow me to introduce myself then. I'm Simon Cordery.'

'And you work for British intelligence?'

Alistair smiled. If she hesitated, he knew he held the upper hand. A second passed. 'Why don't we spend some time together getting acquainted. Anglo-Soviet relations. I know a much nicer place than that bar. There'll be a taxi on the Champs Élysée.'

'And go where?'

'*George V*?' He reached for her arm and draped it over his. They strolled along the street and entered the gardens. He gazed around at the colourful flower beds in the park now illuminated by the pretty ornamental lamps and the delicate evening moonlight. 'There is something so eternally joyful about colourful flowers, even at night,' he said. He glanced at Irina. She was smiling. He turned quickly and reaching down, picked a peony from the garden bed.

'I'm sure you are not meant to do that,' Irina said.

'Perhaps, but they won't shoot me for it. Besides, beautiful women should be adorned with flowers,' he whispered. Every seductive lesson he'd ever learned from Valerie at the Soho brothel came back to him as though it was second nature. An hour later, he held the key to a suite in the famous hotel and ordered several bottles of champagne.

He took the champagne from the ice bucket and popped the cork, then poured two glasses. 'To Anglo-Soviet relations.'

'We've already had that toast.'

'Then to making love in Paris on a sumptuous summer evening.'

'Evening? It's almost midnight.'

'Are you always so pragmatic?'

'Only with men like you.'

Alistair laughed.

'Are you always this forward?' she asked.

'Only with beautiful women like you.'

'Do you always get what you want?'

'Usually.' He raised his glass, 'Do you only ask questions?'

'Why not?'

Alistair laughed again, then removed his coat and threw it over the back of a chair. He moved towards her and taking the glass from her hand, kissed her lips. His hands held her gently, his fingers fondling her check and hair, his lips caressing her neck and shoulders. Slowly, he removed her coat, his hand feeling for the zip in her dress.

'How old are you?' she asked, rolling on her side and covering her breasts with the sheet.

'Twenty-five,' he lied.

'Do they teach how to please women to all recruits in British Intelligence?'

'What a wonderful idea! I'll raise it with my superiors on my return. It should be in the syllabus.'

'Why are you here?'

'Ah! The question of the ages. Why is anyone here, my beautiful Irina?'

'You know what I mean.'

'Same reason you are.'

'I doubt that.'

'Where's Friedleman?'

'Who?'

'Oh, dear Irina. Please don't be coy. It doesn't suit you. You are an intelligent Intelligence Officer. Please don't demean yourself with the innocent act.'

She rolled onto her back and stared at the ornate chandelier hanging from the ceiling above them. 'I don't know.'

He studied her face and believed her response to be genuine. 'So, he's not at the embassy anymore?'

She didn't answer.

'Who were you following tonight? Greaves? Me?'

'You! What is it, your English expression, *you have tickets on yourself*.'

Alistair leaned forward and kissed her shoulder. 'Why don't we run away? Let's go to Tahiti and live the life of beachcombers where we can make love on the sand and swim in warm waters all year round.'

'I am told that sand under the foreskin is very painful. Besides, what would I do with all my rainbow-coloured shoes?'

Alistair laughed aloud. 'Am I to assume by that remark you are willing to defect? It could be easily done. Your car had gone from watching the British Embassy. No one knows where you are.'

'I like my job. And I like Paris. Pour me another champagne?'

Alistair left the bedroom wearing only a robe. He heard her get up and go to the bathroom. He put the glasses on the side table and opened another bottle of champagne. She appeared in the doorway. She had dressed, her coat over her arm. 'I have to go.'

'That is a tragedy. Besides, I have just opened another bottle of champagne. We can't waste it!'

She smiled.

'How will you explain your absence?'

'I will say, I followed you.'

Alistair laughed. 'When will we meet again, my beautiful Irina?'

'It's not so much when we will, but if we will.' She turned to go.

'And you won't tell me where Friedleman is?' he called after her. 'A parting gesture?'

'Not even if I went with you to Tahiti. But, truly, I don't know.'

'Do you know who is with him?'

'I will tell you this. There is a colonel with him.'

'Stasi or KGB?'

'Now that would be telling.'

'From that remark I'll assume he's KGB.'

'Perhaps.'

'Does he have a name?'

She laughed and walked to the door. 'It was a very nice evening. Really.' She opened the door then closed it behind her.

Alistair dressed and left the room. Paying the exorbitant bill, he walked out into the night. His eye searched along the street in both directions for a bar that may still be open. He lit a cigarette, his mind on what he'd learned from Irina Goskova. It wasn't much. But if his hunch about Soviet safe houses being in high foot traffic areas was correct, the left bank suited him. Wandering along the Rue de Rivoli, he crossed the Seine over the bridges that connected the Isle de Cité to the left bank and walked into Place St Michel. Ahead he saw the narrow alley and found number 20, Rue de la Huchette.

CHAPTER TWELVE

Paris

Fri 19th July – Midnight

'Where the hell have you been?' Jenkins said as Alistair entered the tiny flat.

'Furthering Anglo-Soviet relations.'

'And it's taken you two hours to do it? When I was your age...'

'Spare me the details, please.'

'I don't care if you shag the entire universe, just as long as you found out something useful.'

'I could tell you, but then I'd have to...'

'Cut the crap, Alistair.' Jenkins frowned, his annoyance rapidly turning to anger. 'Everything's a game to you, isn't it?'

'Isn't it? Isn't this the best game there is?'

Jenkins rolled his eyes. 'If it is a game, then it's a game that can get you killed. Or worse.'

'Worse? What's worse than being dead?'

'For example, there's being stripped naked and tired to a chair with your testicles in a vice then beaten to a pulp before they kill you, slowly, most likely with electricity and water.'

'Nasty combination.' Alistair shrugged. 'Well, I'm here for a good time, not a long time.'

'I'll remind you of that one day. Well? Did you learn where they've secreted Friedleman?'

'No. And she doesn't know either.'

'You're sure of that?'

'As sure as I can be.'

'So we're back to square one.'

'Maybe. Maybe not.'

'This better be good,' Jenkins added, hoping that whatever information Alistair had extracted from Irina Goskova would placate Grace Quinn. Or at the very least, keep the mongoose from killing him or sending him to the unemployment queue. He sat on the hard wooden chair and pulled his jacket around him. 'I'm listening.'

'Friedleman has a KGB Colonel with him. They'll be somewhere around here.'

'You know that, or you suspect that?'

'I know he has a KGB colonel with him. As to where, it has to be somewhere close by, if they are to keep the appointment at the Louvre on Monday.'

'Did she tell you this colonel's name?'

'No. But if I'd had more time, I would have got it.'

'So, where is she now?'

'Back at the Soviet Embassy, would be my guess.'

'What! What did you tell her?'

'She suspects I work for British Intelligence, but I didn't tell her my real name.'

'Did she say as much?'

'Yes.'

'Is there any chance she was following you, not Sir Richard?'

'I asked her that. She said I had tickets on myself. Besides, if she'd been following me, the car that brought her to the British Embassy would've been outside the Hotel Nice not our embassy.'

'I think we should inform the mon... that is, our former boss.'

'Why?'

'It's just a hunch.' Jenkins stood and wandered towards the window. 'But why is she here? And how is it she can order me to come to Paris? Is she back in charge? Or working for MI6 now? Something involving her is going on. You have to admit that. And, why did Sir Giles send you to make contact with Friedleman? Why did she ask me to keep you in England?' Jenkins lifted the lace curtain over to the window and stared down on the street below.

'Do you expect me to have the answers to all those questions, or are you speaking rhetorically?'

Jenkins remained staring at the street below. 'For what it's worth, Alistair, I don't think she knew Sir Giles sent you to Paris. She's up to something, and maybe it would be wise to inform her of your latest discovery.'

Alistair thought for a few moments. 'While you are in a philosophical mood, Jenkins, have you considered what Greaves said this evening? I don't know about you, but his outburst raised a few questions for me. Do you think he's in on whatever is going on?'

Jenkins let out a long sigh. 'Who knows? But it certainly appears that way.'

'What about Murray, the Legal Attaché?'

Jenkins shrugged. 'What about him?'

'Arrogant bastard, in my opinion.'

'Murray's pretty small fish.'

'Well, maybe we should just ask mother. Do you know where she is?'

'I have a phone number.'

'Get some whisky while you're out.'

'Not a chance. You need to be sober.'

'Well, some coffee at least. I've got a headache.'

'I'm not surprised. All that physical activity will do that!'

Alistair laughed. 'And heres' me thinking you were a virgin.'

Jenkins rolled his eyes and left. He didn't like being treated like the office boy. Or an innocent. Once, he told Alistair what to do. Now Alistair was getting the upper hand. And he'd become arrogant. Perhaps too full of his own importance for his own good. Jenkins knew who Grace Quinn and Sir Giles would blame if anything happened to their golden-haired boy. He sauntered down the stairs, checking if he had some coins in his pocket for the telephone and coffees. He was more than annoyed with himself for allowing Alistair the freedom for what had happened. But what had happened? Perhaps the question was more what was happening? He felt like he was drowning in information quicksand. And none of it made any sense. He stepped into the narrow street and headed for the bar at the end of the lane. He thought about what Alistair had learned from Irina Goskova. And about what Sir Richard had said. Did any of it help to clarify whatever was taking place? Actually, he had no idea. He thought of Grace Quinn and what she would say when she learned he'd left Alistair alone for a few hours. It was a telephone conversation he wasn't looking forward to. He felt the icy chill of the anticipated wrath course through his body as he entered the bar and walked towards the telephone cubicle.

'Ma'am.' Jenkins told her what Alistair had learned.

'Go back to the flat,' she said. 'I'll see you there in fifteen minutes. And Jenkins, you let Alistair out of your sight one more time, you'll be in Wandsworth Prison for the rest of your life!'

Jenkins felt his heart skip a beat. He knew she meant it. He purchased three coffees then returned to the flat and let himself in. He could hear the shower water running as he entered. But to be sure he went to the bathroom to check that Alistair was actually there.

'Would you like to get in with me?' Alistair said.

'Don't order me about! And I'm not a fucking pervert!

'Did you get some coffee while you were out?' Alistair called from the shower.

'Yes. And, I'm not your lacky. Nor am I leaving you alone again. Our former boss will have me eliminated. And, she'll probably get you to do it, too.' Jenkins returned to the sitting room and sat at the small table by the window until Alistair joined him wearing only a towel.

'I could do with a drink.'

'It's coffee or nothing. And you're not going anywhere until your mother gets here and you can explain what happened.'

'She's coming here?'

Jenkins nodded. 'So you'd better put some clothes on.'

'She's seen me naked.'

'You were a lot smaller then.'

Alistair laughed aloud as he headed to the bedroom to dress. 'That was very funny, Jenkins, even for you.'

Fifteen minutes later, he heard the footsteps on the stairs. Given only twenty minutes had elapsed since he'd spoken to her, Jenkins knew that wherever she was staying was close. But why? The nagging doubts swirled. He let out a long breath and went to open the door.

Grace stepped into the grimy room, her grey eyes scanning the small space. 'Well? Tell me what happened with Miss Goskova?' She sat at the table. Jenkins pointed to the third coffee cup.

Alistair walked into the room and went to kiss his mother. He saw her stiffen. Reading her body language correctly, he sat opposite her and told her all he'd learned from the moment he arrived in Paris.

'What would you like us to do?' Jenkins asked.

No one spoke while the mongoose thought. In Jenkins's opinion, even the air was held to attention in her presence.

'You both remain here,' she said. 'And I mean it, Alistair. You move from here without my knowledge, and I'll dispose of you myself.'

'Mother? What's going on?'

'Not now.'

'How can we assist?' Jenkins added.

The steely eyes shifted from Alistair to Jenkins. 'I should think you've both done enough assisting for one lifetime. Stay here. When I need you, I'll contact you. I'll send a runner wearing a black shirt. But you will get little notice. So, I must know where you are. Both of you. Go against this order and you will regret it, I promise you that!'

***

Michail Boyanski was at his desk when Sergei knocked at the door. 'Comrade Boyanski. I have to report that I, along with Comrade Goskova, followed the Englishman Sir Richard Greaves to the British Embassy. Comrade Goskova left to make the telephone call to you, giving me instructions that if a car left the British Embassy, I was to follow it, and she would make her own way back.'

'And?'

'I saw a car leave. A maroon *Morris Minor.* So, I followed it. It went to Les Invalides. I saw a man, not Sir Richard Greaves, leave the car and make a telephone call at a public telephone box. He spent only a few minutes on the phone and returned to the car. I took a photograph of this man. I then followed the car back to the British Embassy. Uncertain if Comrade Goskova had found me gone and had herself left, I decided to return here.'

'You did well, Sergie. Where is the camera?'

Sergi handed it to Boyanski.

'You may go.' Boyanski leaned back in his chair, his hands wrapped around the miniature apparatus, a smile on his lips. He checked his watch. Just after midnight. He decided to have the film developed tomorrow. He stood and unlocking his filing cabinet, placed the camera into the top drawer then resumed his seat, his mind on Goskova. He hadn't received a telephone call from her, so either Sergei was lying or Goskova had acted on a hunch, or something had happened to his assistant. He stroked his chin, the growing stubble irritating his palm. Boyanski reached for his telephone and dialled the extension number for reception. 'Has Comrade Goskova returned yet?'

'No, Comrade Major.'

Boyanski leaned forward. Despite the pleasurable feeling at having the undeniably incriminating photograph in his filing cabinet, he felt the knot in the pit of his stomach he always did when something wasn't right.

***

Ivkin entered the narrow lane that connected Rue Garancière to Rue Palatine and Place St Sulpice. Ahead, he saw a café bar. The owner was outside folding chairs and stacking tables. He hurried towards it. 'Can I buy some food?' Ivkin called.

'We're closed.'

'Just whatever you have left over. My family and I have just arrived from the country, and my child is hungry. Please? Some baguette and cheese perhaps. And some wine, say four bottles? I will make it worth your while,' Ivkin said knowing the man would reopen his till if the amount was tempting enough.

'Ok, I'll see what I have. Wait here.'

The owner went into his shop. While he filled a paper bag with provisions, Ivkin reached for a Paris Match newspaper on a stand by the door and engaged the man in conversation. 'You suffer any damage from the riots?'

'Students!' the barman snorted. 'A bit. A few chairs and tables broken. But no glass, thankfully. They complain about everything. If they'd behaved like that during the war, the Nazi's would have shot them.'

Ivkin took the bag of bread and cheese and four bottles of wine. He didn't want the conversation to continue for too long. Too great a likelihood that the shopkeeper, if questioned could describe him. 'Thanks for the food and wine.'

'Where have you come from then?'

'Lyon. Thanks again. My wife and child will be grateful.'

'You can have that paper,' the man said pointing to what was now yesterday's news.

'Thank you.' As Ivkin left the bar, he noted the telephone in the corner.

Checking the tiny square in front of him, he retraced his steps, his eye scanning the buildings around and opposite for anyone watching from windows or doors from the many apartments in the area. The few who were about were mostly students; young, drunk and disinterested in him. Youth: they were all the same. They coalesced in groups on the footpaths, all searching for cheap restaurants or bars, and engaged in heated political conversation well into the night. And totally preoccupied discovering what the world already knew to notice anyone older than themselves.

Ivkin knocked on the door to the shabby apartment and Friedleman let him in. Ivkin put the bag on the table. 'Anyone come to the door while I was out?'

Friedleman shook his head. 'What did you get? I'm starving.'

Ivkin opened a cupboard and placed two glasses on the table. 'You pour the wine, and I'll cut the bread. It's a simple supper this evening. Nothing like the champagne and caviar we would've had at the embassy.'

'I don't mind what it is, I'm alive. Thanks to you, Grigori.'

Ivkin placed two plates on the table, then cut two thick slices of bread and slabs of cheese. 'Your good health,' he said raising his wine glass.

'And yours, Grigori.' They clinked glasses and Friedleman swallowed the French wine. 'This is very good! You said it was cheap?'

'It's French. They reputedly make the best wine in the world.'

'What a story we'll have to tell our wives on return,' Friedleman said, swallowing more wine. Ivkin nodded and refilled Friedleman's glass.

'Have you worked out what you'll say to Monsieur Benoit on Monday?' Ivkin asked, topping up Kurt's wine glass. He listened as Kurt told him about the sculpture and the photographs he'd brought with him as evidence of the sculptor's genius. He'd heard it all before. Ivkin opened a second bottle, then a third, and they drank late into the early hours of the next day.

Just before two o'clock, Friedleman stood, and Ivkin watched him stagger towards the bathroom. He could hear the stream of urine, then the toilet flush.

'I think I've drunk too much good cheap French wine, Grigori. I must go to bed.'

'Yes. You go. I'll clean this up,' Ivkin said. Standing, he placed the bread into its bag and rolled the cheese in paper and put both into an old refrigerator.

'You're a good friend Grigori,' Kurt slurred.

Ivkin waited ten minutes till he could hear the snoring coming from the bedroom.

***

Grace switched on the light and sat up in the bed. With her right hand reaching for the telephone, her gaze flicked to the clock beside her bed. Three minutes to three. 'Yes.'

'Bill here. *Woodpecker* has made contact.'

'Where?'

'Pont Saint-Michel. Tomorrow, 0600.'

'Right.'

CHAPTER THIRTEEN

Paris

Saturday 20th July -Early Morning

The early morning light penetrated the near empty Parisien streets. Grace left her apartment and walked briskly towards the Seine. On the breeze, she heard the Notre Dame bells ring out the quarter hour. She mused how European church bells sounded different to English bells and for a fleeting moment, she wondered why. Without pausing, she crossed to Isle de la Cité in the middle of the Seine, her footsteps crisp and clear on the pavements. It was still early, too early for tourists or hung-over students. A gentle wind wafted across the river as a small boat passed beneath the second bridge. She checked her watch, then turned right and continued along the near deserted embankment. Turning, she crossed the street and approached Place St Michel. Slowing, she scanned the wide square, her eyes taking in every vehicle and everyone there; assessing what they were doing and where each stood. The only people there appeared to be shopkeepers opening their businesses and delivery vans bringing produce to the many bars and restaurants. Three vans arrived as she stood beside Pont St Michel. Already the morning buzz of enterprise was gathering pace. One kiosk was already serving early customers. She crossed the square and stood in a queue to purchase a hot chocolate, all the while, her eye taking in any movement in the square. Some twenty yards from her, hopeful artists were unlocking their green wooden display cases attached to the Seine embankment hopeful of catching the early customer who wanted the quintessential reminder of the romantic city.

In front of her was the narrow Rue de la Huchette. She hoped Jenkins and Alistair were there and still sleeping off the night before. That Merrick-Smith had sent Alistair to Paris was a complication. Her thoughts momentarily lingered on the young Russian girl, Irina Goskova and what Alistair had learned from her. Taking the hot chocolate, she crossed the square again and stood beside the fountain. Alistair's presence and his contact with the Soviet Assistant was concerning. Grace had spent most of the night awake thinking how Alistair could still be used. She sipped the hot chocolate, her sharp eye on even the slightest movement in the square. But in her mind, she sifted possibilities and ramifications now that Alistair's presence had complicated things. She smiled, a long, slow smile, the sort of smile that comes from the satisfaction of placing the last piece of a puzzle. Perhaps the unexpected situation was a blessing in disguise. And if it worked, and there was no reason it shouldn't, and Alastair continued to behave in his usual predictably, unpredictable manner, they'd get two birds for the price of one.

At two minutes to six, Grace crossed Place St Michel and walked towards Pont St Michel. With thirty seconds to spare, she walked halfway along the bridge and stopped to look at the river below. In the morning stillness, she became aware of the presence beside her. He was like a Doberman pincer, his stealth equally silent and deadly. He was also the only person in the world who could approach her without her being aware of it. And they both knew it. Her skin bristled, and she stood erect, turning only slightly to see his face.

He held a large bunch of pink flowers. 'Don't throw away the wrapping when you dispose of the flowers,' he said, passing the bouquet to her.

She didn't like cut flowers. She especially didn't like pink, cut flowers. She looked directly at him. 'You look well. The cold must suit you. Are you coming in?'

'Perhaps. I'll let you know.'

'When?'

'Tomorrow. 0600 here.'

She nodded.

They separated. Almost in unison. Grace returning to the right bank, the man crossing to the left.

***

Jenkins woke and sat up. He reached for his watch. Not yet six o'clock. He glanced at the bed beside him. Alistair was still asleep.

Pushing his feet into his slippers, Jenkins wandered into the kitchen, then stared out the window to the street below. He saw the local shopkeeper lift the shutters on his shop. Coffee would be nice. Jenkins changed his clothes and took the stairs to the street. Outside, he stared along the street in both directions. It was congested with street vendors and delivery men. But as yet the students were all still asleep.

He wandered along the street towards the square. 'Are you open?' he asked a vendor in Rue de la Huchette.

'What is it you want?'

'Two coffees and two of those pastries.' Jenkins reached into his pocket for the cash.

The clatter of opening shutters filled the narrow street. Jenkins waited while the shopkeeper made the coffees and put the pastries in a bag, his eye scanning the surrounding scene. He then wandered towards the square. Crossing it, he stood by the ornate fountain in the centre of Place Michel. He lifted his gaze as he sipped the strong, hot drink. Opposite and about fifty yards away, he saw a man and a woman standing on the Pont St Michel bridge in front of him. He stared at them. The man held a large bunch of flowers which he gave to the woman. They stood talking for only a few seconds, but there was something about the encounter. Jenkins was too far away to hear what was being said, he could read the body language. They were not familiar in any way, despite the large bunch of pink flowers. But there was familiarity.

Jenkins stood as though dumb.

Even though the woman was a distance away, he knew without question who it was. He felt his mouth drop. He felt spellbound by what he was seeing. The two cups of hot coffee he'd just purchased burned into his palms, but he almost didn't feel it. His throat went dry, but he couldn't take his eyes from what he was witnessing. He swallowed hard, then took another gulp of coffee, burning his tongue, his eyes fixed on the former Director General's back and her distinctive gait as she crossed the Seine with the large bunch of flowers in her grasp. He stared as she stopped by the sandstone balustrade on the far side of the bridge. The flowers were unwrapped, no, torn from their wrapping and thrown into the river below. Stunned, Jenkins looked around for the man she'd been talking to. Turning, his gaze searched the wide square for the man in the dark hat and overcoat. Dropping the drinks, he ran around Place St Michel, staring into the streets that led off the square. Between the vendors and shopkeepers now clogging the place, Jenkins saw the man walking along Boulevard St Michel. He hadn't looked back. Hurrying, Jenkins followed, his eye searching among the growing crowd for the stranger ahead.

Jenkins's mind raced. Who was this man? And why had he met the former Director General? A doubt was forming in Jenkins's head. His thoughts raced too quickly. But they all led to one abhorrent conclusion; was she the rumoured traitor in their ranks? If she was, no wonder she was operating alone. He frowned. Surely that couldn't be correct. In all the years he'd worked for Grace Quinn, she'd never acted alone. In fact, she had been responsible for some of the service's most successful operations. And they always involved numerous people coordinated to the smallest detail. She orchestrated operations. But she was never involved in the execution of those operations. So why was she here now? Was she orchestrating events now? He felt a long, sinister chill, the realisation of the far-reaching arm of MI6. And he almost held his breath. Their presence was like a damp overcoat that never warms. Silent, secret, yet with twists and turns at every corner and very deadly. He ran his hand over his mouth. He wondered if he should call Merrick-Smith. But Merrick-Smith would want to know why he was in Paris. How would he explain it to his current boss that he'd disappeared from London without approval, in order to obey instructions from his former boss?

Five minutes later, Jenkins knew he'd lost sight of the man. The streets and narrow by-ways were now filled with hungry students and shopkeepers, with vans and trolleys congesting the way. Ten minutes later, he returned to the square and purchased two more mugs of hot coffee. The pastries were still in his coat pocket although now more than a little squashed. Jenkins hurried along the street returning to the flat on the top floor of 20 Rue de la Huchette.

'And, I may ask you, Jenkins; where the hell have you been?' Alistair demanded.

'They had to get more coffee from their stores. It took a while.'

'And they asked you to get it?'

'No.'

'Just don't tell me you've been sitting waiting for them to acquire some coffee beans when it's clear to anyone that you've been running. You look dreadful, by the way, like you've seen a ghost. Care to tell me what's going on?'

'I wish I knew,' Jenkins said.

'Meaning?'

Jenkins put the drinks and crumpled pastries on the table and dropped into the nearby chair. 'I don't have the faintest idea.' He ran his hand over his damp brow. 'Why are you even in Paris?'

'Odd question, even for you, Jenkins. Merrick-Smith told me to come and make contact with an East German scientist named Friedleman. I was to get to know him and find out what I could about what he's working on.'

Jenkins leaned forward, with his elbows on the table, he cradled his head in his palms. 'It just doesn't make any sense.'

'What doesn't?'

'Remember that letter you brought to me at Leconfield House? It was from your mother. I was to keep you in England for the next two weeks. And she isn't happy I didn't.'

'Right! So, it would appear that Merrick-Smith doesn't know what's going on either. Anything else I should know about?'

'I'm as much in the dark as you are, Alistair.'

'I doubt that! Tell me Jenkins, do you know why mother is here?'

'I don't know that either.'

'Did you tell her I was here?'

'No. She knew.'

Alistair leaned back in the chair. 'So, who told her?' he said, half to himself.

Jenkins shrugged. 'Maybe Merrick-Smith. Has to be. Perhaps Sir Giles told your mother directly about you.'

'Unlikely. She would have told him to keep me in England.'

'Either way, Merrick-Smith now knows we're both here. And Greaves would've confirmed it. How am I going to explain this?'

'The real question, Jenkins, is why are our masters keeping secrets from each other?'

'I'm beginning to feel like a pawn.'

'Welcome to my world.' Alistair paused, then lit a cigarette. 'We may be pawns, as you put it, but mother is the queen. And a queen can move in any direction, remember.'

'You don't need to tell me that!' Jenkins sighed heavily. 'If Sir Giles and your mother both want Friedleman, why are they acting independently?'

Alistair drew on the *Gallois* and blew the smoke into the air. He watched it dissipate. 'Smoke.'

'What?'

'Smoke. What if Friedleman is a smoke screen.'

Jenkins stared at Alistair. 'I think I should tell you about something I've just witnessed...'

Alistair sat listening while Jenkins told him what he'd just seen on the Pont St Michel.

'It was definitely mother you saw on the bridge?'

'No question.'

Alistair drew on the cigarette again, then scratched his chin. 'What are they up to? If Merrick-Smith wanted me to make contact with this East German, he must be thinking of snatching him. Not that that was my brief.'

'Well, it wasn't mine either.' Jenkins paused. 'So whose job is it, if that's what they have in mind?'

Alistair shrugged. 'So, why aren't they talking to each other? And why did MI6 ask for someone at MI5 to come here and not send one of their own? And I don't buy that bit about wanting an unknown. Surely they have plenty of their own.'

Jenkins was silent for a few seconds. 'You've heard the rumours about a mole in MI5? Well, is it possible...'

'If you mean my mother could be the traitor, you've really lost the plot. She has MI5 in her genes. She eats, sleeps and thinks MI5. She may have married and had children, but the love of her life is The Service. That is, if she is capable of love. No one else comes even close. Not even her children.'

Jenkins was nodding. 'I know. It was just a thought.'

'A stupid one. Even for you.'

'And if Friedleman is a smokescreen?' Jenkins said at length. 'Then what's it about?'

'Something bigger? Well, let's call her and find out.'

'My God! She'll be apoplectic.'

'Nothing I haven't seen before. Give me the number.' Alistair left the flat and walked to the bar with the telephone at the end of the narrow street and dialled the direct line. After three rings, a woman's voice answered.

'Mother?'

There was a brief silence. 'Alistair.'

'I think we should talk.'

Another pause. 'Alright. There's a patisserie near you on the corner of Rue de la Huchette and Place St Michel that opens early. Be there at *exactly* ten minutes to six o'clock tomorrow morning and bring Jenkins. And that, Alistair is an order.'

'Why so early?'

He heard the line disconnect.

***

The telephone rang. 'Grace? What news?'

'I have something.'

'Anything I should know about?' Bill asked.

'Not over the phone.'

'And the bait?'

'Everything's in order. Just make sure that back up team is in place.'

'They're set to go. Grace, you do know the Soviets will be out looking for him. Especially if they believe he's defecting.'

'Understood.'

'Right! When?'

'Tomorrow. 0600.'

CHAPTER FOURTEEN

Paris

Saturday 20th July – Mid Morning

Michail Boyanski sat at his desk in his office on the ground floor of the Soviet Embassy, his gaze settling on the vast blue sky outside his window. He could see it was a beautiful day outside, the morning appeal of summer in Paris. But it didn't matter which city he was in, he didn't share the day's bright optimism. His gaze shifted to the stern portraits of Stalin and Khrushchev on the wall opposite his desk. The bright summer's day instantly vanished from his mind and all he felt was the forbidding pall of judgmental faces and his impending harsh fate. Something about the proceedings of last night's cocktail party and the timing of events weighed on his mind. That the British and Americans would want Friedleman stood to reason. But he felt confusion; an emotion that wasn't familiar to him. While Friedleman and Ivkin's arrival in Paris and their subsequent hasty departure from the embassy appeared genuine, his gut instinct was raging. He worried if he was overreacting. He hadn't been forewarned of anything untoward from KGB headquarters in Moscow. He picked up the telephone receiver and dialled the number of the safe house in Rue Rillon near to the Pantheon in the Fifth Arrondissement.

'Madame Gillot. I wish to speak with Colonel Ivkin.'

'I was expecting him last night, Comrade Boyanski, but he didn't arrive.'

Boyanski felt a flood of alarm course through him. 'Why didn't you telephone me!'

'I thought they were held up with the street barricades. And I didn't want to bother you if they were just delayed. I was about to inform you that they hadn't arrived.'

'Not good enough Madame Gillot! You had better hope I find them.' He slammed the telephone receiver down and stared at the portraits. But his brain was in free-fall. He stared into the air in front of his face as he recalled every detail of the previous evening and the order of events. Ivkin and Friedleman had left the embassy around 19:00 not long after the party had begun. But despite Ivkin saying he'd call when they were in the safe house, Boyanski hadn't heard a word from Ivkin either from the safe house or anywhere else for that matter. He pondered if they'd been followed or something had happened to one or both of them to maintain silence for so long. He looked at his watch. Fifteen hours of silence, in fact, and his intuition was telling him something was very, very wrong. He ran his tongue around his dry lips. And now there was another complication; Goskova had failed to return. It was so unlike her. But although Goskova not returning was concerning, it was Ivkin's and Friedleman's whereabouts that dominated his thoughts. His chubby fingers thumped the armrests of his chair in frustration. He stared at the telephone on his desk. But with no real evidence to the contrary, whether it was the whereabouts of Goskova or Colonel Ivkin and Friedleman, it was still a gut feeling, and he didn't wish to involve the French Police based purely on suspicion. At least, not yet. Grabbing the receiver, he lifted it to his ear and dialled the extension for the garage. 'Sergei?'

'Major Boyanski.'

'Come to my office immediately!'

'Is something wrong, Sir?'

'Just come when you're told!' Boyanski bellowed. He banged the receiver down then stood and paced his small office.

Minutes later, Boyanski heard Sergei's heavy tread outside his office before the knock on his door. Boyanski sat down again. 'Come in and shut the door behind you.'

Sergei did as instructed.

'Did you take Colonel Ivkin and Comrade Friedleman to the safe house last night?'

'I did, Major,' Sergei paused. 'Well, not to the house exactly.'

'What the hell does that mean?' Boyanski roared.

'There are still a lot of students protesting in that area. Colonel Ivkin said, if we were being followed, he didn't want us leading our enemies to our safe house. The crowds were thick, Major Boyanski. We couldn't have got away easily if anyone was tailing us. This sounded reasonable to me, so I did as he requested. Besides, he's KGB, and I have no wish to offend a colonel of the KGB.'

Boyanski leaned his elbows on his desk, his large hands rubbing his face. 'I am KGB, you idiot! Now stop prattling and tell me where you saw them last?'

'The Luxembourg Gardens.'

Boyanski glared at Sergei. 'Get out!' he screamed, his voice resonating around his small office.

'Do you need me any further today, Major?'

'Go to hell for all I care! And shut the door behind you!'

Sergei spun on his heel and left without further comment.

Boyanski stood and poured himself a double vodka. His hands were shaking. More from rage than fear. Swallowing it back in one gulp, he thought of the people involved in last night's sudden removal of the East German scientist: Goskova, Ivkin and Friedleman and the idiot Sergei. Unlocking his filing cabinet, he withdrew the guest list for the previous evening's event and placed it on his desk. His gaze fell on the list of names. Sir Richard Greaves had been a last-minute invitee to the cocktail gathering. Boyanski rubbed his chin. He felt the panic taking hold. And the cold web of uncertainty, a toxic cocktail of suspicion and conspiracy. It was all-encompassing and all invasive. He didn't believe he was a stupid man, but a thought was developing in Boyanski's mind. Goskova, he excluded. In the two years she'd worked for him, she'd never given him a moment's cause for suspicion. But where was she? He stroked his fatty chin, the frustration growing. He needed answers. Boyanski sat again at his desk and breathed deeply, then lifted the receiver and dialled the number for the garage. 'Sergei?'

'He isn't here, Major Boyanski. It's Ivan, the mechanic speaking.'

'You'll do. I need you to drive me to Place de la Madeleine.'

Twenty minutes later, Ivan pulled the car up beside the green huts the flower sellers use in Place de la Madeleine, and Boyanski got out. 'Wait here. Or if you need to move, just circle around. This won't take long.'

Boyanski opened the door to the bar and stepped inside. To his left was the long wooden bar, a spectacle of polished timbers, gilt mirrors and sparkling crystal. A barman wearing a waistcoat and black bow tie stood behind it.

'Did a young women with blonde hair come in here late yesterday wanting to use the telephone.'

'Maybe. You her father?'

'Don't be impertinent!'

'Who then?'

'Her employer,' Boyanski said.

The barman eyed Boyanski. 'Yes, she was here.'

'Did she use the telephone?'

The barman shrugged.

'How long did she stay?'

'Not long.'

'You saw her leave?'

'No. She left by the rear.'

Boyanski frowned. He knew Goskova would only have done that if she thought she was being followed. 'Was anyone with her?'

'There was a persistent young man. He bought her champagne.'

'Do you know his name?'

The barman shrugged again. 'Another man came in looking for him. That man called him Simon.'

'Did either of these men leave with the girl?'

'No. Are you going to order a drink?'

'No. Here.' Boyanski threw a hundred francs on the counter and left. He stood outside on the footpath and waited for Ivan to pull up. The barman's information, if it was true, hadn't helped him locate Goskova. But at least she'd been astute enough not to engage with this unknown young man whose name was probably not Simon.

'Where to, Major?' Ivan asked.

Boyanski thought for a few seconds. He thought about Goskova and where she would have gone after leaving the bar. She could be anywhere, and he had no intention of driving all over Paris looking for her. But she had discerned the young man as a possible threat and had evaded him. All Boyanski could do now was wait for her to make contact. 'Back to the embassy.'

The car sped away from Place de la Madeleine. Knowing that Goskova had tried to make the telephone call was reassuring. She evidently wanted to get away from this Simon and had left before making the telephone call to him at the embassy. As troubling as her whereabouts was, the fates of Colonel Ivkin and Friedleman concerned him more. Their disappearance could see him returned home with more than a tarnished reputation. Losing a KGB colonel and a valuable scientist on his watch could see him stripped of his rank and most likely sent to the labour camps. He pondered Ivkin's concerns for the scientist's safety. Had he been correct about someone following the Soviet car? Were they in hiding? Or, had they been abducted? If they had been snatched by the British or Americans, then both men would be taken out of France. Boyanski thought about the two men who'd followed Goskova. If they were British or American intelligence officers, Goskova would be leading them on a merry chase around Paris. Boyanski smiled.

He returned to his office on the ground floor of the embassy and sat behind his desk. It was a waiting game. A game he had never liked. He looked up at the stern face of Stalin, a man no one crossed and lived. While abduction of Colonel Ivkin and Friedleman was a real possibility, instinct told him they were still in France. Captured or in hiding, he had to find them. He drummed his fingers on the desk. If they left the car near the Luxembourg Gardens, then it was most likely they were still in the area. 'They'll be somewhere in that rabbit warren around St Sulpice,' Boyanski muttered to himself. 'But I do know one thing; if they are still here and able to do so, Friedleman will not miss that appointment on Monday. He talks of nothing but this wretched sculptor.'

Boyanski rested his hand on the telephone, his fingers lightly tapping the receiver. He should inform the Ambassador. But informing the Ambassador would mean a report to Berlin and Moscow, and he didn't want that. Not yet. Boyanski stared again at the portraits of the current and past presidents of the USSR on the opposite wall. 'Why?' he muttered, not daring to voice his doubts above a whisper. Why had he not heard from Ivkin? Boyanski's gaze returned to the blue skies. 'But...' he paused, the fingers of his left hand stroking his protruding chin. A chill ran down his shoulder and arms until it coursed over his entire body. 'Is it possible?'

Boyanski stood, then walked over to his filing cabinet and unlocked the second drawer. He felt his jaw tighten. He rummaged through the drawer, the action becoming more frantic by the second, but the brown leather pouch containing the Makarov PM pistol was gone. So was the box of ammunition. He thought back, trying to remember the last time he'd used it. Or seen it. The drawer was always locked, and he had the only key. How could it have disappeared? Then he remembered he'd left Ivkin alone in his office last night when he'd taken Friedleman to the side door of the embassy. His mind dwelt on Ivkin, a respected senior KGB colonel. That Ivkin could be an impostor was unthinkable. But asking for confirmation of Ivkin's identity would alert Moscow, and there would be an enquiry. If asked, he'd say he was just doing his job thoroughly. Yet, it had the potential to end his career. Or skyrocket it. It couldn't be helped. He needed to know. He pushed the filing cabinet drawer shut and strode to the communications room in the basement. He burst into the room, the communications clerk jumping to attention at his sudden arrival.

'Send an urgent message to KGB headquarters in Moscow. Tell them I want a current photograph of Colonel Grigori Ivkin, and I want it now!'

'It will take us a few minutes to send, Major. It has to be encoded.'

'I know that! Just get on with it! This is top secret and urgent. Give it the highest priority.'

'Major.' The cypher clerk set about encoding the message then typed it ready for sending.

'How long before we have an answer?' Boyanski demanded.

'As it's Saturday, they should deal with it as soon as it arrives. But it may take longer to retrieve the photograph.'

Boyanski glared at the young cypher clerk.

'If it is marked urgent, we should have an answer within a few hours, Major.'

'You'd better hope so!' Boyanski said and stormed out of the communications room. Boyanski took the stairs from the basement. He felt the escalating rage fed by frustration and rising anxiety. A few hours. Fifteen hours had already passed without contact. Despite his hunch that Ivkin and Friedleman were still in Paris, the reality was that they could be anywhere. And his urgent request for a photograph of Colonel Ivkin would raise eyebrows. He needed to tread carefully to avoid not only the ambassador's but also KGB Moscow's censure and their combined reactions to Ivkin's and Friedleman's disappearance. He pondered again informing the ambassador, to enlist his help but knowing the man's volatile temper, Boyanski knew he needed accurate information before doing so. He contented himself that Ivkin had encountered some form of trouble, and was simply lying low. Perhaps taking the pistol had been purely a precaution due the recent civil unrest in Paris. If that were the case, alerting the French authorities could jeopardize their safety and embroil the USSR embassy in unnecessary publicity. Something his masters at KGB headquarters would not appreciate. And, sounding the alarm too soon without accurate intelligence would cause more harm than good. Especially to himself. He stared at the files on his desk, but his mind wasn't on them. Only the whereabouts of Ivkin and Friedleman occupied his thoughts, and with each passing hour, he became more anxious. He turned his mind again to Goskova. He rang the officer on duty at the front gate, but still Goskova had not returned, nor had she telephoned. He rubbed his chin again.

It was early evening when Boyanski telephoned the French police. He tapped his desk as he waited for the response from the officer on duty at Paris Gendarmerie. That no young blonde woman matching her description had been brought into the City Gendarmerie alive or dead in the last twenty-four hours, didn't make his anxiety any less. In his mind, he tossed about possibilities. He could only think of two: she'd been randomly abducted and possibly killed or held captive by a local criminal or she'd been taken by force by either or both of those men she'd met at the bar and was being held captive. But why? What did she know? Was it purely lust? She was beautiful. He checked himself wondering why he'd thought in the past tense. Perhaps she'd been abducted because she could identify Friedleman and Colonel Ivkin. But that presupposed whoever had taken her knew who she worked for. But if Ivkin and Friedleman had been taken by the West, then Goskova's capture served no purpose.

Boyanski swung the chair around and stared at the ceiling. At least he'd had some good news. The film which he'd had developed from the miniature camera Goskova had given to Sergei while watching the British Embassy was now safely locked in his personal filing cabinet.

A knock at his door intruded his thoughts. 'Come!'

'We've had a response from KGB Headquarters in Moscow, Major. The photograph you requested, Major.'

Boyanski stood and snatched the teleprinted photograph of Colonel Grigori Ivkin from the cypher clerk. He felt an instant wave of relief. Although grainy from the transmission, it was Ivkin, and it proved beyond any doubt that Ivkin was who he said he was. Boyanski also hoped the KGB colonel never learned of his doubts. He reached for the telephone and phoned the garage.

'Where's Sergei?' Boyanski bellowed.

'He said you sent him away, Major.'

'Not for life! However, if he keeps this up, it could be. You'll have to do. Come to my office.'

'Now?'

'Yes, now!' Boyanski waited only minutes before there was a knock at the door. Ivan walked in and stood before Boyanski's desk.

'This is a photograph of Colonel Ivkin. He is with another man, a scientist from East Berlin. They are somewhere in that maze of degenerates around St Sulpice. Find them! I don't care what you have to do, just find them. And don't come back till you have, do you understand?'

'It may take me some time to find them, Major.'

'Start with bars and food shops. Show them the photograph.'

'And when I do locate them, should I telephone you?'

'Yes. No matter the hour. And you better take a weapon with you. I'll telephone the gunroom and arrange for you to have a pistol. But do nothing other than surveillance. And, only use the weapon in an emergency. If you see them or learn where they are, telephone me here immediately.'

Ivan left Boyanski's office. Going to the underground armory, he collected a pistol then, grabbing his jacket from the drivers' room, drove away from the embassy.

***

From the window of the top floor flat, Ivkin watched the young, dark-haired man walk in and out of several shops and bars before disappearing into the tobacconist directly opposite. He wore jeans, rolled up at the cuff, an open-neck shirt and pointy-toed black leather shoes. He also wore a red bandana around his neck. Ivkin watched this figure linger around the adjacent tobacconist. Five minutes later he was joined by another. This person also wore jeans rolled up at the hem along with a hat that concealed their head and face. Ivkin stared at the two people as they talked for a few minutes then parted each going in different directions. The next twelve hours were critical. And the most dangerous. The deception would take precision as well as all his skills. And more than a little luck.

***

Boyanski sat mulling over events. Several hours had passed, and he hadn't heard from the mechanic. With every passing minute, valuable time was wasting, but he didn't really know what else to do. He tentatively reached for the telephone receiver then dialled the number. He waited for the familiar voice to answer. 'Any news?'

'Why are you phoning me?'

'Do you know where Ivkin and Friedleman are?'

'Aren't they with you?'

'No.' Boyanski relayed the events of the previous evening.

'I'll make some enquiries.'

'Have you seen Irina Goskova?'

'No. Don't telephone me again. I'll call you when I have news.'

Boyanski replaced the receiver in its cradle. The conversation had yielded nothing of use and served only to anger a most valuable informant. Boyanski stood and paced his small office. His mind conjured possibilities. But the maze of options served only to make everything more confusing. When the telephone on his desk rang, he jumped at the sound. His hand reached for the receiver. 'Yes?' he snapped expecting to hear Ivan's voice.

'Major Boyanski?'

'Speaking.'

'This is General Moshenko of Moscow Central Committee.'

Boyanski stood erect, his heart pounding. 'Comrade General. How may I be of service?'

Boyanski listened, his pulse rate increasing. 'It will be done immediately.' Boyanski replaced the telephone receiver and sat heavily. He'd never received a call from so high an authority as Moscow Central Committee. And, for the first time in his life, he felt vulnerable. Not knowing the whereabouts of Friedleman or Ivkin now made carrying out Moscow Central's orders more than difficult.

But the order was clear.

Boyanski sat motionless for half an hour, his pulse rate high and his palms sweaty. Standing he walked towards the bureau in his office and poured himself two double vodkas then swallowed both in quick succession. He sat again at his desk, then reached for the telephone and dialled the number. 'I know what you said, but I need to tell you something important.'

'You've found them!'

'No. But I do have someone out looking for them. It's not that.'

'Before you tell me, I think you should know, you are not the only one looking for the East German scientist. There's an arrogant young man in Paris. Sent by British Intelligence to make contact with Friedleman.'

'Really?' Boyanski thought of the two men in the bar who'd most likely followed Goskova. 'Is he dangerous?'

'Only to himself. Leave him to me.'

Boyanski cleared his throat. 'I have just received orders from Moscow Central...'

There was silence at the end of the line as Boyanski imparted the message.

'Are you there?' Boyanski asked.

'Yes. Do you know why?'

'A missing note book which held sketches of his latest invention.'

'You cannot seriously expect me to ask questions about this. The minute I even tried to enquire I'd be suspected. They just have to be found. And when you do, call me.'

***

The telephone rang. 'Sorry to disturb.'

'Are they in place?'

'Yes.'

'Where?'

'In an apartment in Rue Garancière.'

'Good. Stay watching. Anything untoward, call me. And be careful. A lot is riding on this.'

***

The telephone in Boyanski's office rang. He stared at it hoping it wasn't General Moshenko or anyone from Moscow Central again. His hand slowly reached for the receiver.

'Major Boyanski, I've located Colonel Ivkin and Herr Friedleman.'

'Comrade Goskova! I'm so pleased to hear your voice. Where are you?'

'Latin Quarter. I saw Colonel Ivkin buy some food in a local shop and I followed him. I'm watching the apartment he went into from a nearby hotel.'

'You can tell me how you came to be in the Latin Quarter later. I'll come now. And Comrade Goskova. You have done well. But why you didn't return to the embassy?'

'Major, I couldn't. I was being followed. I managed to lose him in the back streets around the Sorbonne. Do we have a safe house in Rue Garancière?'

'No. Colonel Ivkin was correct. They must have been followed. It's the only explanation. Irina, don't make any contact with them until I arrive; it will only expose them. If our enemies are watching Colonel Ivkin, the minute they leave that apartment they'd be abducted. Stay watching. I'll come straight away.'

'Major, if I may, do not come now.'

'Why?'

'We don't know if they are alone in the apartment. If there was an altercation, and gun shots were heard, it would certainly attract the local police. Then the Ambassador would be involved, the world's press and the security services of The Soviet Union, Britain, France and any other embassy whose citizens may be present. It would be very public.'

'Goskova, there is something you don't know.' Boyanski drew in a deep breath. 'I received a telephone call from Moscow Central Committee earlier. I have been ordered to eliminate Friedleman.'

'What? Why?'

'Not for you to know.'

'And Colonel Ivkin?'

'No. Just Friedleman.'

'Then it must be handled covertly. Major Boyanski, we could use this situation to incriminate the West. Then no suspicion could fall on us or our Mother Country for the death of Herr Friedleman. His assassination in Paris would be a major embarrassment to the Western Allies. It should be in a public place. Not in secret in an apartment.'

'What you are suggesting is bold, but if we could pull this off, Moscow Central would be very pleased. Tell me what you are thinking, Goskova?'

'If Friedleman were killed publicly, with lots of witnesses, the West would be blamed for permitting the killing of a Soviet citizen. It would reflect badly on the French. And the British or Americans would be blamed. They would then all suspect each other. It would undermine their trust in each other.'

'It is a good plan, Goskova. A daring one. But what about Colonel Ivkin? If he were killed, there would be huge ramifications for us.'

'If Colonel Ivkin were inadvertently killed, that would be even more damaging for the West, Major.'

'Yes. Very good. Alright. Tell me how you think we should play this?'

'I'll stay here watching. Colonel Ivkin collected some food late tonight. But it wasn't much. Just one bag. That tells me they are not moving tonight. So, he is either going to move location tomorrow or, if they are being held, whoever is holding them will move them in the next twenty-four hours. Because it is now late, I'm guessing it will be early tomorrow morning before too many people are about. When they move, I will call you. That way we will know if they are being held captive. If they are alone, I will follow them and telephone you when I can.'

'If they are alone, I need you to tell me what they are wearing and in which direction they are walking. I'll have a car on standby to speed across Paris the moment you call. If they leave by car, get the registration number of the car. But Irina, don't get involved. You may be injured.'

'I will do as you say, Major.'

CHAPTER FIFTEEN

Paris

Sunday 21st July – Early Morning

A car horn woke him. Alistair swung his legs over the side of the bed then went to the window. Below two vans were blocking the narrow Rue de la Huchette, neither driver prepared to back up. Within minutes, the drivers were standing in the street shaking fists at each other. The altercation had drawn a small crowd. Alistair watched, studying the body language and wondering who'd give in first. His money was on the bigger of the two men. But his need for coffee was more pressing than knowing who'd win the battle for Rue de la Huchette. He returned to the bedside table and reached for his watch. Half past five. Attaching it to his wrist, he went into the other bedroom. Jenkins was still asleep. He nudged

Jenkins awake. 'Hurry up. We have to be in Place St Michel in twenty minutes.'

Jenkins moaned and rolled over. 'It's Sunday. Go away.'

'Want to stay in bed? Ok, you deal with mother when you don't show up.'

Jenkins groaned then sat up, throwing the sheet and blanket off then rubbed his face. 'Ok. You win. At least we can get some coffee there.' Jenkins stood and reached for his clothes then walked into the bathroom. 'What are you going to say to your mother?' he shouted.

'What about?'

Jenkins appeared naked in the doorway to the bathroom. 'About what I saw on the bridge; her and that man in the overcoat and hat.'

'Nothing.'

'Nothing? Aren't you the least bit curious about her clandestine rendezvous with a stranger?'

'Mother told us to be in the square at ten to six. Rather a specific time, don't you think? And Dame Grace doesn't do random. You should know this. She will have her reasons,' Alistair said, pulling on his shirt and jacket. He felt in his coat pocket for his pistol and checked it. Reaching for the box of ammunition he'd received in the parcel from Jean, he put six loose bullets along with the box in the other pocket of his jacket.

'You're expecting the gunfight at the OK corral?' Jenkins said.

'Just being prepared. As I said, Mother doesn't do random.'

'Somehow I don't see you as a boy scout.'

'Not a boy scout. Just someone who is naturally suspicious, as you should be. And, someone trained to be prepared by a sadistic Scott.'

'Ah, yes. Sergeant Major Cox.'

'The same. Once met, never forgotten,' Alistair said momentarily wondering if the callous Scott was still bullying Service recruits in the freezing wastelands of the Scottish Highlands. Jenkins left, and Alistair heard the water running in the shower. His mind recalled the hardened visage of Sergeant Major Cox. It was during his time there Alistair had learned to shower and dress in less than five minutes. It wasn't the only lesson he'd learned in the wilds of Scotland.

Alistair flopped into the armchair by the window while he waited. Four minutes later, Jenkins appeared, and they left. Locking the door to the drab apartment, Alistair preceded Jenkins down the stairs to the street. He opened the entry door to the building and looked out in both directions before stepping into the alley. The fresh, cool morning air drifted along Rue de la Huchette. Around him, the morning ritual of opening businesses was in full swing, and the two arguing van drivers had gone along with their vehicles. Alistair rummaged in his trouser pocket for a few francs. As they walked towards Place St Michel, a rather pleasant, sweetish aroma wafted on the breeze. Alistair and Jenkins strolled towards the open kiosk ahead in the wide square. Off to his left and beside the large fountain, a flower vendor had set up a tiered trolley of brightly coloured flowers under a red and white striped awning. Alistair stared at the vendor. The man looked more like a weightlifter than a flower seller. Alistair felt his heart skip a beat, and his instinct kicked in. 'Do you have a pistol on you, Jenkins?'

'Always. Why?'

'I'm getting the impression that something is about to happen.'

'Really? What makes you say that?' Jenkins said, his gaze darting around the square, his eyes focusing on the windows and doorways of the surrounding buildings.

Alistair nodded towards the muscular man and his flower cart. 'Rather large biceps for a flower seller, don't you think? I'll get the coffees. But I wouldn't take your eye off him.'

Jenkins crossed Place St Michel to the middle pavement where the fountain dominated the square. Set between two of the many streets that converged at Place St Michel, the area had several bench seats placed in front of the fountain and facing Pont St Michel and the Seine. Jenkins chose one with a good view of the square. He sat down, his back to the fountain, his head half turned away from the muscular flower seller in front of him and slightly to his right.

Alistair hurried towards the kiosk but kept the flower seller in his peripheral vision. While he waited for the coffee, he saw the man arrange the displays of violets along with daisies and roses and other blooms he couldn't name. The man's actions, Alistair could see, were as unfamiliar to the role of flower seller as heavy-weight prize wrestling was to a three-year-old. And, from what he could see, Alistair believed the enormous hands were more accustomed to the grip of a machine gun than delicate springtime blooms. Alistair carried the steaming aromatic coffees towards the bench where Jenkins was sitting. He handed one to Jenkins. As he sipped the strong brew, he scanned all the surrounding buildings, the windows that overlooked the square, the streets that led off it, and the bridge over the Seine. But he saw nothing unusual. If it hadn't been for the flower seller, he wouldn't have suspected anything. But the predictable, ordinary routine of the place had him on edge.

Jenkins took a sip. 'What do you think is going on?'

'I've no idea. But with Mother involved, I suspect we'll soon know, and, for some reason, she wants us here.'

***

'Kurt, wake up!' Ivkin shook Friedleman's shoulder.

'What is it, Grigori?'

'We have to leave. It's no longer safe here.'

Friedleman sat up quickly, his eyes wide. 'What's happening?'

'Get dressed. And wear a coat. It's early. Here take mine,' Ivkin said removing his coat and handing it to Friedleman.

'Aren't you coming with me?'

'Yes, of course.'

'Won't you need your coat if it's cool out?'

'It's alright. I'm not cold. But we should go soon.'

Friedleman stood. Hurrying to the bathroom, he quickly dressed and pulled on Ivkin's coat. 'Where are you taking me? Do I have time to pack my suitcase?'

'No. Just leave everything behind. I'll get it later. But wear a hat. Here, take mine.'

'What's happened?' Friedleman said pulling on Ivkin's hat.

'I'm moving you to a safer place. Then I must inform Boyanski of my suspicions and that I've moved you. I'll collect your things from here then. We are being watched, Kurt. Come. Look.' Ivkin held back the flimsy curtain over the window. Do you see that man down there standing in the doorway to the tobacconist?'

'Isn't he just a customer?'

'Don't be naïve, Kurt. He's been there for the last ten minutes pretending to read newspapers and magazines. But he's watching the door to this building.'

Friedleman stepped back from the window. 'What's happening, Grigori? I thought this was a safe house?'

'It is. But last night I think I was followed back from the shop after buying the food. And there is only one person other than Major Boyanski who knows we are in a safe house in this vicinity.'

'Who?'

'The embassy driver. I suspect he may be a British agent. But we must stay one step ahead of him.'

'My God! That Englishman at the embassy, Sir Richard Greaves. No wonder he was so polite.'

'Polite? How? What do you mean?'

'He asked me all sorts of questions.'

'What questions?' Ivkin snapped.

'Mostly about the sculptures.'

'Nothing about your work at home?'

'No. But he did ask if I lived in East Berlin. Did I do wrong?'

'What did you say? Think, Kurt. What exactly did you tell him?'

'He said he knew Berlin and asked where I lived. I said I lived near the Majakowski Ring.'

Ivkin stared at Friedleman. 'You may as well have told him you work with East German Intelligence.'

'But I don't!'

'He doesn't know that.'

'Is that man still there?' Friedleman asked, his nervous eyes darting to the window.

Ivkin checked the street, then turned to face Friedleman. 'Yes. I must ask you now not to speak to anyone.' Ivkin paused seeing Friedleman's anxiety. 'It will be alright. We'll be away from here soon. As soon as he goes inside the shop to pay for that newspaper he's holding, we'll leave. Now hurry. We don't have much time. And keep my hat pulled down over your face. I'll wear your hat.'

'But they might mistake you for me?'

'Then they'll kidnap me, and you'll be alright.'

'I can't let you sacrifice yourself like that for me.'

'There is no time to argue, Kurt. Just do as I say, and we'll both be fine.'

'I'm so sorry, Grigori. You're a real friend. Your willingness to put yourself in danger for me proves it. I should never have doubted you. I apologise wholeheartedly. Do you think the appointment will still happen on Monday?'

'I hope so, Kurt.'

'Where am I going?'

'We'll be met on the Pont St Michel at exactly 6am. So we must hurry. A woman carrying a bunch of violets will ask you the time. Go with her. She'll take you to another safe house on the Right Bank. As soon as I am certain no one is following us, I must inform Boyanski and see that the driver is interrogated. Now come.'

Ivkin led Friedleman down the stairs and quietly opened the door to the street. He peered out through the narrow opening. He waited until he saw the man holding the newspaper walk into the shop. 'Now. But, Kurt, don't run. I'll go first. Walk no more than ten paces behind me.'

Pushing Friedleman through the door, Ivkin led him down Rue Garancière towards Rue St Sulpice.

CHAPTER SIXTEEN

Paris

Sunday 21st July – Early Morning

Alistair took the cups back to the vendor and ordered two more coffees. While the café owner prepared the hot drinks, he kept one eye on the flower seller and the other eye roaming the square, buildings, doorways and windows. Taking the drinks in both hands, he wandered back to the bench where Jenkins sat. On the morning air, he heard the bells of Notre Dame chime six. At exactly the same time, and directly in front of him, Alistair saw her crossing Pont St Michel. She crossed the road and without stopping, walked straight towards them, but did not make eye contact. In fact, she didn't acknowledge either Jenkins or himself. She paused by the flower seller and bought a bunch of violets. Alistair was immediately on high alert. He knew his mother's dislike for cut flowers. She turned and stood no more than two yards from them, fumbling with the change and putting her money purse into the handbag over her shoulder. 'Stay here,' she whispered. 'Do not get involved in anything you see unless I instruct you. Do I make myself *crystal* clear,' she emphasized through gritted teeth. Her gaze shifted to Jenkins. 'That includes you. Phone me in one hour.'

'What's going on, Mother?'

'Not now.' She walked away, heading back towards the bridge. Alistair and Jenkins waited. Draining the last of his warm coffee, Alistair placed his cup under the bench, but his gaze was fixed on his mother. A minute later, two men wearing unseasonally heavy coats came out of Rue Hautefeuille, the narrow street beside and behind him. Jenkins stood. Neither moved nor spoke. Alistair stared after them, his hand going straight into his pocket, his fingers gripping the pistol secreted there. One man was about three yards in front of the other now. He wore a hat, so Alistair had not seen his face. He felt a small, contained smile spread across his face. His mother never failed to disappoint. He believed he was watching Herr Friedleman and his KGB minder. Alistair slipped the safety catch on the pistol still in his pocket, his gaze glued to the two men. He flicked a glance at Jenkins. Jenkins was on high alert, his hand in his pocket, his feet spread apart. They waited. Neither spoke. Alistair watched as both the men walked briskly across the square then appeared to be heading for the bridge. Neither stopped.

At that exact moment, a long black Mercedes with darkened windows, sped around the corner from the Quay des Grands Augustins adjacent to the Seine, the tyres making a repetitive juddering ripple as the vehicle sped over the cobblestones. With a squeal of brakes, the car came to an abrupt stop in Place St Michel. It waited only a second before it swung right at speed, the tyres spinning on the uneven pavement. At the sound of the screeching tyres, both men stopped as though stunned. A second later, both started to run towards the bridge. But the car reversed with a squeal and stopped between the two men on one side and Grace Quinn now standing on the pavement beside the bridge. Then the rear car window half opened. Alistair saw both men fall to the street. He stared in horror expecting the men to be shot where they lay. It was as though time was standing still. But he could see that neither man was shot nor in any way injured at this stage. Alistair pulled the pistol from his pocket. He flicked a glance to his mother. Was this all part of her plan? His gut told him it wasn't. He stared wide eyed as the muzzle of a rifle protruded through a rear window of the car. It was pointing towards the prone men in the square. He felt his mouth fall open. He stared transfixed, almost unable to breathe. He couldn't believe they were just lying on the ground waiting to be shot. Surely there had to be a reason for their actions. From the bridge, Alistair saw his mother holding a pistol. It was raised and pointed at the car. Without waiting, Alistair and Jenkins upturned the bench seat, and kneeling behind it raised their pistols. Alistair let off two shots, both hitting the car's side panels. Alistair saw the muzzle shift sideways towards him. A quick burst of shots was fired, but they fell short of where he and Jenkins were positioned, hitting and pinging off the street. At the sound of the gunfire, the flower seller pulled a machine gun from the flower cart and began firing over the heads of the prostrate men at the car, the rapid staccato of bullets from an automatic weapon ricocheting off the cobblestones, hitting the car's side panels and puncturing one of the car's rear tyres. The car's bullet-proof window closed. As soon as the machine gun had started, one of the prone men rolled away from the gunfire. Alistair watched. The flower seller's machine gun wasn't trained on the prostrate men. The muscular flower vendor was there for protection and unforeseen circumstances. Another hallmark of his mother's preparedness. As soon as this barrage of gunfire started, one of the fallen men pulled the other to his feet and together they ran towards a *Colonnes Morris.* But the tall onion-domed advertising column was not designed for protection. Both men stood rigid behind the tall, rotund structure as volleys of shots rang out from the car, pinging the cobblestones and shattering the glass in the advertising column. Surrounding him, people were screaming and running in all directions. Peering around the edge of their makeshift barricade, Alistair stared at the scene, his eyes wide and unblinking. He didn't believe his mother had planned such a shambolic and very public extrication. Despite her precautions, something unexpected had happened. His gaze shifted to his mother who still stood on the other side of the black car and beside the Pont St Michel. His heart was racing. Before him, he watched his mother run from the bridge, the pistol still in her grip. Alistair held his breath as he raised his L9A1 again, Jenkins doing likewise. Grace ran across the street that ran parallel to the Seine and positioned herself beside the first building overlooking the square. But Alistair knew she hadn't fired. Doing so would draw the assassin's attention. Alistair's focus shifted to the two men who still sheltered behind the shattered Morris column. One was holding the other, possibly preventing him from fainting or just to stop any unpredictable actions caused from rising panic as the bullets flew around the wide square.

Mayhem had broken out in Place St Michel, but Alistair was no longer aware of the crowd's screams. The rapidity of events unfolding around him deadened the senses. The car's rear window opened again, and Alistair saw the muzzle of the automatic machine gun protruding once more from the darkened window. A frenzy of machine gun fire now coursed across the open square, the bullets spitting off every surface. The screaming had stopped. Place St Michel had emptied. The cacophony was replaced by a palpable silent terror from those who hid in the nearby streets and buildings. The flower seller stood wide-legged beside his flower cart and unleashed his weapon, sending streams of lightning flashes of bullet fire across the square and hitting the body of the car. The strident rapid fire pinged off the cobblestones, and the car's side panels. The car windows were riddled with the telltale concentric pattern of gunfire on the bulletproof glass. Standing, Alistair held his pistol with both hands, and levelled it, firing at the half open car window. The bullet bounced off the shiny surface. The gunman inside the car now pivoted the machine gun towards Alistair once more. Jenkins lept forward pushing Alistair down as a volley of shots pierced the surrounding air. Jenkins fell to the ground as the flower seller kept up the barrage. With that, the car surged forward, the rear window closed. 'Get who's in that car!' Grace shouted as she ran into the square. She pointed at the disappearing black car as it sped into Rue de la Huchette, the tyres now shredded and sparks coming from the metal wheel rims grinding on the cobblestones. Alistair looked around. In the distance, he thought he heard the sounds of approaching sirens. Jenkins was down, clutching his left arm, his shirt stained red and blood pooling on the road beneath him. 'Are you badly hit?' Alistair called. Jenkins sat up still clutching his left arm. 'Go! It's nothing! I'm fine. Go! Go!' Alistair scanned the scene.

In all the confusion, a motorcyclist had pulled up by the fountain. The rider seemed paralysed with fear, unable to move. Alistair rushed towards him and pushed the cyclist from the seat. Pushing his pistol into his belt, he jumped on the motor-cycle and revved the engine, and without waiting for further instructions from his mother, sped into Rue de la Huchette. As he left the square and from the corner of his eye, he saw the two men leave the protection of the Morris Column and hurry towards the bridge. His mother had joined them there. All three hurried away heading towards Ile de la Cité. He guessed his mother had just kidnapped Friedleman and his KGB minder. But what he hadn't seen was resistance from either man. That only raised myriads of more questions. As he sped along the narrow street after the damaged black car, he pondered the identity of the man with Friedleman and what part his mother played in it all? But perhaps the more important question was who in the car wanted Friedleman and his minder dead? The sirens sounded closer now. He hoped Jenkins had got himself back to the apartment on the top floor and well out of sight from the local gendarmes. Alistair wove his way along the narrow street, students and shopkeepers jumping aside, their fists shaking, their voices raised in anger. He saw the black car ahead, heading for the bridge to cross the Seine. It wasn't hard to spot with the flashes of orange sparks coming from the metal wheel rims. People in vehicles surrounding it were calling out, but the driver took no notice. Despite the mayhem, Alistair felt the untimely smile return. It spread over his face, and he had no wish to disappoint his mother. 'Don't fuck up now, Quinn!' he shouted at himself as the traffic surged forward, and he dodged a van. In his head, he replayed the events of Place St Michel. So much planning and preparation. Even though he believed the arrival of the black bullet-proof car wasn't part of his mother's plan, she had placed the flower seller there. She'd anticipated trouble. No more than that; she'd expected it. But, if everyone wanted the East German scientist, who wanted Friedleman dead?

Keeping the car in sight, Alistair swerved through the traffic on Quay de Montebello running parallel to the Seine until he saw it turn left onto the Pont de la Tournelle where it stopped, caught in traffic. He slowed the motorcycle and put two cars between himself and the black car, his eyes glued to what was happening. He knew that with the tyres now shredded and gone and the car running on metal rims, it couldn't make it back to Boulevard Lannes many miles away. 'I have you now,' he muttered, his eyes fixed on the vehicle. The traffic began to move forward. Over his left shoulder he heard the high pitch sound of an approaching 50cc motorcycle. It sped past him, weaving between the cars and vans. It carried a driver and a passenger, both wearing helmets. Alistair saw it pull up beside the car. His mouth fell open as he held his breath. 'Surely not!' he said, his voice only audible to himself. Such blatant assassination attempts in public places were not the modus operandi of either the British or the Soviet secret services. It was more like a gangland execution. Unless desperation had orchestrated it. He stared at the moped rider and passenger. Whatever was happening, he couldn't tell if it was planned or spontaneous. The passenger got off. Alistair could see it was a woman. She removed her helmet then opened the rear door of the car. A big man got out and put on the black Paris Geno helmet. Her companion, the motorcycle rider, also got off the bike and handed his helmet to someone still seated in the car. When another man emerged from the black car, he was already wearing the head covering. Both men quickly then jumped onto the moped and sped off. The exchange had taken less than a minute. Alistair racked his memory for anything familiar about any of the men. But nothing about either man — from the car or the moped driver — was familiar to him. The woman, however, he knew immediately even without her rainbow coloured stiletto high heeled shoes. She, along with her companion, left the stranded car and building traffic jam with irate drivers, and walked nonchalantly across the bridge, hand in hand as lovers do. 'Oh Irina! What are you up to?' Alistair whispered to himself. But the Soviet Assistant Intelligence Officer wasn't his quarry. At least not yet. Dismissing any thoughts of Irina and whoever was with her, Alistair kept his eye on the 50cc moped ahead. Weaving his way through the traffic, and following at a distance, they entered Place de L'Etoile. The bike was some way ahead of him now, and as more motorcycles entered the chaotic whirlpool, he lost sight of it in the congestion.

***

The telephone in Boyanski's office rang.

'Yes.' Boyanski knew the extension number was for the front gate.

'Major, Comrade Goskova had just returned. I thought you'd want to know.'

Without further discussion, Boyanski hurried to the side entrance. He met her in the side hall. 'I have been worried about you, Irina. Come to my office and tell me what you've learned.'

They walked without speaking to Boyanski's office. Irina sat in front of Boyanski's untidy desk.

'Major Boyanski, before I tell you what I've learned both before and since our brief meeting on the bridge, tell me please, what happened in Place St Michel?'

Boyanski stood and paced his office. 'The simple answer is, I don't know. He should be dead. Of course, Colonel Ivkin doesn't know about the death warrant Moscow Central Committee have ordered for Herr Friedleman. But I'm sure my contact isn't that bad a shot that he missed Friedleman every time. As soon as Ivan returns with the car, I'll check the weapon. It must be faulty.'

'But it didn't jam. It fired. So why is Herr Friedleman not dead?'

Boyanski's face contorted. 'Why, indeed!' Boyanski continued to pace. He stopped and faced her. 'You were there? In Place St Michel?'

'Yes. I told you I was staying in a hotel in the area. I was watching them. All night. I saw them leave, but there was no time to locate a telephone to telephone you. But you didn't tell me why Moscow Central wants one of our top scientists dead?'

'I suppose it no longer matters if you know.' Boyanski paused and drew breath. 'Apparently he brought sensitive documents with him from East Berlin. He intended to defect.'

'How did they learn this?'

'Colonel Ivkin telephoned his superiors on the day Friedleman crossed the border to West Berlin and reported it. That was how he could come to Paris at such short notice.' Boyanski paused. 'And now they are both in the hands of the British or the Americans. My career is over. I'm ruined, Goskova.'

'And Friedleman is not dead,' she said, half to herself.

There was a long pause. 'Yes. So it would seem.' Boyanski sat heavily in his chair then leaned back, his gaze on the ceiling. 'I shouldn't have agreed to let them go to the safe house.'

'Is the assassin you engaged reliable?'

'My God! Is it possible he deliberately missed?' Boyanski stood suddenly, shaking his head. 'I don't believe it! I won't believe it! He has been supplying information to us for years. Valuable information. Although he was as amazed as I was by Moscow Central's order.'

'Reliable or not, it may no longer matter. The simple fact is that Friedleman is still alive, and the only glimmer of hope is that he is still with Colonel Ivkin.'

'Let's hope so, Goskova. If the British find out about Ivkin, they are both lost to us.' Boyanski slumped again into his chair. He leaned forward on the desk and held his head in his palms. 'My career is over, Irina but I will try to minimize the fallout on you.'

'Major. It may not come to that. I'm sure Colonel Ivkin will do everything in his power to protect Friedleman and attempt to escape as soon as he can. It's too late for self-recriminations. There must be something we can do.'

He looked at Goskova. 'You are a loyal colleague, Goskova. But I will have to take responsibility for their capture.'

'Perhaps there is still time. We must find them and get them back here.'

'You have a plan?'

'Perhaps.'

'Unless we can think of something, I will be returned to Moscow and executed.'

'No, Sir. I will not let that happen. You are a good officer and do not deserve this. I'll do it. I'll find them,' Irina said.

'How?'

'I found them once I can do so again.'

'I haven't heard from Ivan the mechanic. I sent him out to look for them. Actually, in all that's happened, I forgot about him. Perhaps you and he could join forces.'

'Where did you send him?'

'Around St Sulpice.'

'I'll find him. We can work together.'

'I thank you for your loyalty. But, I repeat, how will you do this?'

'There is a young British Intelligence Officer called Alistair Quinn. I know where he gets information. I'll leave a message for him to contact me. He thinks he is such a ladies' man. But he has made a big mistake. I know his weakness. It is his ego. And he finds me attractive. I will use this.'

'Was this the man in the bar who followed you?'

'Yes.'

'How sure are you that he'll contact you?'

'There is nothing more certain, Major Boyanski. And because he thinks he can manipulate women, he will attempt to seduce me. Then he will ask for information. But it will be I who will direct the conversation, and I will learn where Herr Friedleman and Colonel Ivkin have been taken.'

Boyanski slowly nodded. 'Comrade Goskova, perhaps you can be of extra service to our country. I have heard of this young man before, this Alistair Quinn. He may not be as gullible as you think. And it could be he means trouble. To us. To you. I am authorizing you to eliminate this man, this Alistair Quinn, as soon as you locate him and of course, carry out the orders of Moscow Central. Can you do it?'

Irina nodded. 'Of course, I can do this, Major Boyanski. I, like you, trained for just such circumstances. Enemies of our state are not to be tolerated. But not poison this time. It takes too long to take effect. A silenced weapon, I think.'

'I want to recommend you for the highest award for bravery and ingenuity, Comrade Goskova. Without your courage and timely assistance today, there may have been a very different outcome. And although it didn't go as planned, your actions were of the highest standards of devotion to the Soviet Union. And to me personally. But tell me now how you were there on that motorcycle?'

'After I left here yesterday evening, and as you requested, I followed Sir Richard Greaves to the British Embassy. When he didn't reemerge, I went to telephone you from the bar in Place de la Madeline. There I met this British agent, Alistair Quinn. I thought it too coincidental that he was in the bar. Without making it obvious, and so as not to lose him, I did not make the call to you but instead, left the bar by the rear. I knew he would follow. But when he didn't find me, I followed him and another man to a flat on the left bank. I decided to watch them, hoping they would lead me to Herr Friedleman and Colonel Ivkin. Then, as you know, I saw Colonel Ivkin, so I followed him to Rue Garancière. The rest you know. I saw what happened in Place St Michel. I convinced a young French student to assist me. I'm going to meet him again tonight. I want to make sure he is still unsuspecting about what really happened there.'

'And if he is suspicious?'

'The Seine is fast flowing.'

Boyanski sat in his chair, his big head nodding. 'The highest honour I can request for you.' Boyanski stood and walked towards a cabinet behind his desk. Taking two shot glasses from the cupboard, he poured the vodka into both glasses and handed one to Irina. 'I know it's early, but your courage and ingenuity should be celebrated.' He turned to face Goskova then raised his glass. 'Your good health and congratulations on a job well done. If only more showed such devotion and foresight. To you!' Boyanski swallowed the liquor in one gulp. He put the glass on his desk. 'But I have grave fears for Colonel Ivkin. If the British do have them, Ivkin is the greater prize. Of course, they would have to know his importance, or he'd have to tell them, which he would only do under much duress. He is a brave and resourceful officer. This young Frenchman on the motorcycle, how did you convince him to help you?'

She smiled. 'It wasn't hard. I said the man in the car was my father who works in the government. I said he had an important meeting and needed to get to the Hotel du Ville. With the car's tyres damaged, if he loaned my father and his secretary his motorcycle, I would arrange for him, and a group of his friends who are still protesting about the changes at the Sorbonne, a meeting with my father. He agreed. I'll meet him later tonight and give him a thousand francs which, of course, he will take as a consolation for me being unable to arrange the meeting. But I will also confirm his disinterest in the events on the bridge.' She paused. 'Do you know you were followed?'

'By whom?'

'A British agent on a motorcycle.'

'Do you know who he is?'

'Yes. The British agent you mentioned; Alistair Quinn.'

'How do you know this?'

'I saw him behind the car. He probably saw the transfer on the bridge. But he has never met you, and he wouldn't have seen your informant's face. So, he cannot really do any harm to us. And soon he won't be able to.'

'You will be taking a very big risk, Irina. Are you sure you can do this? A honey trap followed by an assassination, in fact, two. This is difficult for a seasoned operative let alone a young woman.'

'I will do my duty, Major. But perhaps I could request that you send Sergei to follow me. That way, if I need help, he is not far away. And should anyone detain him, or question him for whatever reason, he knows nothing of our plans.'

CHAPTER SEVENTEEN

Paris

Sunday 21st July 1968 – Morning

Grace stayed ten paces ahead of Ivkin and Friedleman. They crossed the Seine at Pont St Michel then slowing, strode on, crossing the Seine again over Pont d'Arcole from Ile de La Cité to the Right Bank. They hurried along the road parallel to the Seine and towards the wide square in front of Notre Dame. They didn't stop. Striding on past the cathedral's open doors and gathering tourists and onto the far side of the vast cathedral. In the narrow street beside the northern side of Notre Dame, Grace slowed to a walking pace then stopped beside a café. She paused, her gaze scanning the shops and windows in the immediate area. She stared at Friedleman's face. She could see his terror. Her eyes coursed over the man's body looking for any sign of injury. There was no evidence of physical trauma. She spoke in German. 'Are you hurt, Herr Friedleman?'

'No. I don't think so.'

'Good. We need to keep moving. The gun shots will attract the local police, and soon they will cordon off this part of Paris,' she said.

'I'll leave you here,' Ivkin said. 'Kurt, stay with this woman. She is completely trustworthy. And you will be safe with her.'

'Grigori? You're coming back though?'

'Yes, Kurt. But I must go now.'

'When you can arrange it, we will be at this address.' Grace handed him a scrap of paper with the address of the apartment on the Right Bank. Ivkin memorised the address and handed the note back. Grace switched to Arabic, fairly certain that Friedleman wouldn't understand. 'Don't be too long. We have to get you both out tonight.'

Ivkin nodded continuing in Arabic. 'We need proof. Irrefutable proof.'

'Will you get it?' Grace asked.

'I think so. But keep him locked up. He's frightened, and fear will make him unpredictable.' He turned again to Friedleman and switched back to German. 'You are safe now Kurt. She will look after you until I return this evening.'

'What language were you speaking to this woman? What are you keeping from me?'

'You are right to be suspicious, Kurt. Especially after what has just happened. But she isn't German. She's Egyptian, so she only has limited German.'

Friedleman nodded, but Ivkin could see the skepticism.

'I'll be back soon. Don't worry. Everything will be alright,' Ivkin reassured him. Ivkin glanced around the area, then straightened his coat and hurried away.

Grace and Friedleman watched Ivkin march away, back towards the open square. 'We should go,' Grace said in halted German. She felt a sudden pang of fear for Ivkin; an emotion almost unknown to her. 'Colonel Ivkin is a brave man, Herr Friedleman. Now we must do our part. I have an apartment not far from here. But we should leave now.' Ushering Friedleman along the footpath she led him across Rue de Rivoli and ten minutes later, they turned into Rue Ste-Croix de la Bretonnerie, and Grace escorted him to the first floor apartment. They stepped inside, and she relocked the door behind them. Friedleman stood in the middle of the reception room. Grace saw his expression. With its silk curtains and plush furnishings, it was grander than anything Friedleman would have ever seen. 'Herr Friedleman. Would you like some tea? Or would you like something to eat? A drink, perhaps?'

'Is this a safe house?'

'Yes.'

'It couldn't be more different to the one Grigori took me to.'

'I'm sure. Colonel Ivkin is frugal. He doesn't like Western ostentation. But I think you will be more comfortable here. Won't you sit down?'

Friedleman kept his gaze on Grace.

She smiled in response.

'Thank you. With all that's happened, I would appreciate a drink. Some schnapps or vodka, if you have it. Then I'd like to know what's going on.'

'Of course.' Grace went to the bureau beside her small desk and poured the liquor. She passed it to him. 'Please, do sit down.'

Friedleman sat down in the luxurious satin covered chair and swallowed the drink whole.

Grace sat at the small desk by the window. 'Another?'

'Not yet. Not until you tell me what I want to know.'

'Very well. What I'm about to tell you will surprise you, Herr Friedleman.' She opened the top drawer of her desk and withdrew a pistol then laid it on the desk by her right hand. She glanced at Friedleman. She saw his eyes widen.

'Have no fear, Herr Friedleman. It is for my protection, not yours. But I will use it, if you try anything.'

She saw Friedleman's heightened apprehension.

'What's going on? Who are you?' Friedleman said dropping the empty glass down on the table beside him. He stared at the glass. 'Have you drugged me?'

'I have not drugged you, and my name is irrelevant. But the life you had in East Berlin is over. You are heading for a new life in the West, Herr Friedleman. Freedom. And, if you wish, I will do my best to get your wife out of East Berlin.'

Friedleman stared at her, his mouth open and his eyes wide in astonishment.

'That's correct, Herr Friedleman. Your friend Grigori Ivkin works for British Intelligence. In MI6. But the attack on you and him this morning was not part of our plan. So someone else is interested in you. But they are not trying to capture you, they want to kill you. And that can only be your own people; the Soviets. We in the West want you alive.' Grace opened the drawer again and withdrew a small notebook. 'Could it be that they have learned about this?'

Friedleman's eyes widened further, and his face blenched at the sight of it. 'My God! How did you get that?'

'Colonel Ivkin. I told you he works of us.'

Friedleman stared at the book as the realisation struck. '*He* stole it! He took it to implicate me with the Stasi. Why did he do that?' Friedleman shook his head. 'Such betrayal! Grigori, a spy! A British spy!'

'He lives a very dangerous life, Herr Friedleman. However, he is also a very careful and thorough man. But how he got your notebook no longer matters.'

'He is a traitor and a thief!' Friedleman stood suddenly, his jaw clenched, and his face florid with anger.

'That thief risked his life to save yours. And not just today! From where I stand, your reaction to him getting you to freedom doesn't seem very grateful, Herr Friedleman.'

'Grateful! He lied to me. To Marlis. He said he was a backroom clerk. Then I learn that he also works for the KGB. Now this! Our friendship was a sham! Does his wife, Ludmilla know? How can I trust him, any of you? How have you done this?' Friedleman slumped into the chair and slammed his fists onto the satin armrests. He shifted in the chair and no longer able to contain his anger, he stood then paced the room. 'No.

Don't answer that. I don't want to know right now. I'm too angry to take it in. Such betrayal! Years of betrayal!'

'Ivkin has endangered not only his life several times for you already, but he is doing so again, now, in an attempt to learn who tried to kill you this morning. Those are the actions of a very brave man. He is risking the Soviets discovering his own deception so that you can have freedom. If they discovered his true allegiances, he'd be taken back to the USSR under guard and shot. And I could do little about it.'

'Are you telling me the attempt on my life this morning wasn't part of your plan to kidnap me?'

Grace poured herself a gin and tonic. 'That's exactly what I'm saying. It was not us. I would never condone something so conspicuous. My guess, Herr Friedleman, is that once your masters learned about your missing notebook, they assumed you brought it with you to the West in exchange for asylum.'

'And Grigori used this to his advantage! Because of him, I can never return.'

'I'm glad you recognise that.'

'Everything Grigori has said is a lie. Everything I've ever believed about him is a lie. So, why should I believe you? A person I've never met till now. I don't trust anything you say.' Friedleman paused.

Grace retrieved his glass from the side table and poured another vodka. She handed it to him, holding his gaze as he reached for the glass. His hand was shaking.

'Does Ludmilla, his wife, know?'

Grace paused, then sat down again.

Friedleman's face blanched. 'My God! She doesn't know about him. What sort of person does this? Who are you people? Or maybe you've been lying so long you no longer know.'

'Trust him one last time, Herr Friedleman, and we will get Marlis out too.'

'Why should I believe you? You planned this whole thing! You and Grigori.' Friedleman drained the glass and putting it on the table beside him, slumped back into the chair.

'It doesn't matter what you think of him or me. You are free, Herr Friedleman. Free! Free to do whatever you wish and go wherever you want. That is, once I have you out of France and a new identity is created for you. And, if you stay calm and do as we say, I will get your wife out too.'

'And Ludmilla! His wife. Is she to come too?'

'She isn't his wife.'

'I was at his wedding!'

'It doesn't count. He's already married.'

'Wha....! Kurt couldn't finish the question. 'My God! Who are you! What are you?'

***

The telephone rang.

'What news?' Bill Trant asked

'He's with us.' Grace responded.

'And *Woodpecker*?'

'Soon.'

'Do you need further backup?'

'No. Give me another twenty-four hours, and we should have them all. I'll see you in London.'

'Well done. I think you may be included in the next honours list. Baroness Grace Quinn, perhaps this time.'

***

Ivkin waited in a recessed doorway to a shop. It was still early, not yet eight o'clock. While he couldn't be certain, he felt sure no one had followed him and Friedleman to the Right Bank and no one seemed to be loitering in the nearby streets. He visualised Friedleman sitting in the apartment in Rue Ste-Croix de la Bretonnerie. He would feel betrayed. But when his anger subsided, he could also feel excitement. It had been decided that Grace should inform him of his new life in the West. Friedleman wasn't his problem now, and he needed to focus on who had been behind the attempted assassination. He pondered the identity of the killer. He had two suspects, but until he had further concrete information, it could be either of them. He closed his eyes and recalled every detail of the failed assassination attempt; where everyone was when the car suddenly arrived and what then ensued. With both Friedleman and him lying flat on the road, they were an easy target. The action had been decided by Grace in case of unforeseen circumstances so that the flower seller could use the machine gun without risk of hitting them. So, with such an easy target, why had the assassin missed? If he was the intended victim, then Moscow Central had learned of his true identity. In his gut, he didn't believe it. If he'd been the target, Boyanski would have involved KGB assassins, and they used less obvious means of elimination or, if the victim was to be shot, they didn't miss. The target had to be Friedleman, and the attempt had been organised by Boyanski. But why? Fleetingly, he wondered if Grace was the intended victim. He dismissed that option almost immediately; the gunman had pointed the machine gun into the square not towards the bridge or the nearby building where Grace had secreted herself. Ivkin leaned on a railing fence of Pont des Arts and scanned everyone around him. Police were still on the Left bank. But nothing there would be learned or discovered. MI6 clean up teams were quick, thorough and professional. And never caught. He glanced at the activity in Place St Michel. Gendarmes were on all the pavements stopping people and questioning them. And it wouldn't take them long to learn from the shopkeepers about the two men who'd hidden behind the Morris Column who'd then disappeared across the bridge to the Right Bank. Being the hunted wasn't a familiar role for Ivkin, but he enjoyed the anonymity of it. Satisfied no one was taking interest in him, he walked on. Walking was good. He breathed in the scents of the river, the fragrance of the air in summer and even the occasional birdsong in the plane trees. Such times gave him time to think. He knew he needed to sort facts from suppositions. When he faced Boyanski, nothing could be left to chance. Ahead he saw a café. He hastened towards it. Inside, he ordered coffee. From his seat by the window, he stared at the river and the passersby as he replayed the events of the morning over and over in his head. The black car. He replayed its arrival in the square like a rewound movie; the way it had suddenly appeared, the squealing brakes, the abrupt halt and the use of a machine gun and not a sniper's rifle. He sipped his coffee. With Friedleman now removed, assuming he was the intended victim, no further assassination attempts would be forthcoming. But that wouldn't stop them from wanting to locate the scientist. In fact, Boyanski would turn Paris upside down trying to find him. Ivkin visualised Boyanski; the unleashed temper, the rage of not knowing where Friedleman was. But what had prompted the bungled attempt? That the assassin had missed them both at such close range worried Ivkin. Was it just the unexpected presence of the MI6 flower seller with the machine gun near his floral cart? Either the assassin in the car was a terrible shot or... Ivkin frowned. He needed some answers. If the Soviets suspected him of helping Friedleman to defect, returning to Boulevard Lannes would see him returned to the USSR and executed. But what of Friedleman? Ivkin knew enough about Soviet KGB procedure that unless the West gave Friedleman a new identity and a legend, he would be killed, silently and lethally by an injection of Ricin, or something equally lethal, chemicals so powerful that just a few drops would see the victim become emaciated and dead within weeks. That Friedleman would be living in Britain or America didn't stop the Soviets from carrying out the murder of those they considered traitors. Even if it took years. At least, the British had Friedleman for now, and soon he'd be out of France. But the identity of the leak at MI5 or MI6 remained unknown. Ivkin felt they were close. Suspicions about the identity of the British Intelligence leak was one thing, absolute proof quite another. Ivkin sifted information in his head. An idea was forming. And Boyanski was the key.

Ivkin left the café and crossed the Seine at Pont Neuf his senses on high alert. He then doubled back to wait on the other side of Ile de la Cité. From where he stood, he could see Place St Michel. The local police had blocked off the streets to all vehicles around the small square. But there appeared to be no evidence of what had happened there earlier in the day except the many indentations made by bullets hitting the sandstone structures and pavements. He'd seen the backup team arrive in a white van in all the confusion as he'd left with Friedleman. And they had done their work; and all traces of the incident removed. Even the carpet of strewn flowers was gone. Except for the excited police, a degree of normality had returned to the small square. He crossed the square and lingered around the shops, buying a packet of cigarettes and watching who came and went in Rue de la Huchette. Using the narrow thoroughfare, he pulled his hat down on his head and slowly walked away, blending into the inquisitive crowd. He saw no one suspicious, but then curious eyes usually watch from behind drawn curtains. And all the windows that faced the street were shops, restaurant or cafés, not apartments.

Strolling now, he walked towards Rue St Jacques and taking the back alleys, crossed the Seine at Pont de l'Archevêché. The great Cathedral of Notre Dame loomed over the city, a silent witness to the tumultuous events Parí́s had witnessed for hundreds of generations. Taking the Pont d'Arcole he crossed to the other side of Ile de la Cité. There was no sign of anything unusual, and Grace and the terrified Kurt Friedleman had long since gone. He ambled towards the Tuileries Gardens and sat on a bench, then checked his watch. To any passersby, he was a tired old man snoozing on a garden bench. But his mind processed everything he knew and speculated about what he didn't. Thirty minutes later he strolled towards the Champs-Élysées and took a taxi to Boulevard Lannes.

***

Alistair parked the motorcycle outside the police station in Place Vendôme and where he knew the gendarmes would remove it most likely returning it to its hapless owner. His eye coursed the large square. People and vehicles. But no one just standing, watching. He didn't expect there to be. After all, stealing the moped and following the black car hadn't been planned. He stood on a corner and hailed the first taxi he saw. 'Place de la Madeleine, merci.'

Alistair paid the fare, then crossed the square and stood on the pavement outside the Madeleine church. He lit a cigarette, his gaze on the bar opposite. He felt as much in the dark as he'd ever been. What he needed was a drink and information. 'You ought to be used to it,' he chastised himself. Being kept in the dark was a familiar childhood experience. Lessons learned from two decades ago and nothing had changed in nigh on twenty years. But returning to inform his mother that he'd lost the men on the motorbike would not endear her to her firstborn. Dodging the traffic, he hurried towards the bar in the top corner of Place de la Madeleine. Relieved it was open, he pushed the door wide. Jean was behind the counter. He looked up as Alistair entered.

'Café, monsieur?'

'Whisky. Double.'

Jean's eyebrows raised, but he didn't comment on the early hour. He picked up a glass and poured the single malt which Alistair felt sure was the most expensive whisky in the place. He didn't care. He needed the fortitude it gave him.

'You've had a difficult morning, I think, monsieur?'

'You could say that.'

Jean leaned on the counter. 'I have a message for you.'

'Really?'

Jean nodded. 'From a young woman who uses my telephone on occasions.'

Alistair swallowed the liquor and placed the empty glass on the counter. 'Well?'

'She wishes to meet you. Tonight, at the hotel. She didn't say which, but I suspect you know.'

'Did she say a time?'

'Nine.' The barman paused then reached for the bottle again. 'Another?'

'Why not. Has anyone else asked about me?'

The barman shook his head. 'Not in person. But I am to give you a piece of advice, monsieur.'

'Which is?'

'Go home John Pevington.'

Alistair swallowed the drink then putting the money on the counter stood to leave. The message ricocheted around his brain. *Not in person* could only mean Jean had received a telephone call. From where? That was the question. But perhaps that wasn't the right question. Perhaps it was a case of English punctuation; was it *Go home, John Pevington* or *Go home John Pevington*. One interpretation was a threat, the other a warning. 'Who left this message for me?'

The barman shrugged. 'It was a man's voice on the telephone.'

'Any accent?'

'English. Maybe.'

'How did you know the message was for me?'

The barman shrugged. 'I don't get many English customers collecting handguns from me. Perhaps I am just a suspicious man. But, with this now and your attraction to our young and beautiful Russian friend, and that you have at least two names that I know of, well. It can only be you, n'est pas?'

'Why do you think I have two names?'

'At least two. Simon Cordery who collects parcels. And John Pevington, who should go home. I'm also sure neither of these names are really yours. I'm also sure you have any number of them, monsieur.'

'And you don't know who left that message for me?'

'As I said, an English sounding voice on the telephone.'

'Male or female?'

'Male.'

'Old or young?'

'Difficult to tell. Not young. Not old.'

'Very helpful! That describes half the population of Paris.'

'I'm sorry I can't be of any more help, monsieur.'

'I wouldn't say that. I think, Jean, that you are a font of information. It's just a matter of price.'

Alistair left the bar. He wondered if the barman had passed on this message to anyone else. But even if he did inform Irina or any other employee of the monolith in Boulevard Lannes, it didn't really tell them anything. He meandered along the narrow footpath heading for the Champs-Élysées and any bridge to cross to the Left Bank. He felt total confusion. Not an emotion that was familiar to him. He thought about Jenkins and wondered if he'd sought attention for the flesh wound on his arm. He suspected Jenkins would have returned to the flat to lick his wounds and to await further orders like the good little soldier he was. Alistair checked his watch. It was now almost midday. Friedleman, Alistair assumed, would be safely tucked up wherever his mother intended him to be. But who was the other man? For Friedleman to have been with him, the man must have at least been known to Friedleman. Or, Friedleman trusted him. Did that mean this other man was a Soviet? He remembered what Jenkins had told him about his mother and a man meeting on the Pont St Michel. But as he had reminded Jenkins, his mother ate, drank and slept MI5, so she knew him. Soviet or not. She knew him. 'More unanswerable questions,' he muttered. Alistair reached for his packet of

Gitanes, lit it and inhaled the heady tobacco. What game was his mother playing? While he knew MI6 had long arms, his mother's were longer. Or she had more of them. But getting information from his mother if she didn't wish to answer his questions would be impossible. Grace Quinn could keep her mouth more tightly closed than a Pharaoh's tomb. And he couldn't get the answers from her the way he usually did with women. The image in his head was that of Irina Goskova and her beautiful naked body lying on the crisp snow white sheets of the *George V*. He thought about Irina and wondered about her reasons for wanting to meet him. Was it just sex? If not, then what game was *she* playing? She came across as naïve, an accident waiting to happen. Although for her to be working for Boyanski she had to have some skills beyond good looks. Perhaps Alistair thought, he'd underestimated her. For her to be rescuing assassins on the streets of Paris proved she was more than a low-ranking junior officer of limited experience. It also proved those assassins were Soviets. But why they should want Friedleman dead was a mystery which he couldn't answer.

He left the bar and walked towards Rue Royale. Off to his right, he saw a taxi pull up, and a smartly dressed, mature aged woman alighted. Holding the door for the woman, he extended his hand to assist her from the cab, keeping the door open. The woman smiled. With the door still open, he sat in the rear passenger seat. 'Place St Michel,' he told the driver. They crossed the Seine at Pont de la Concorde and turned left, following the river.

Traffic congested the road ahead. Quai des Grands Augustins was at a standstill. 'I'll walk from here,' he said to the driver. Paying the fare, Alistair jumped out and pushed his way through the crowds that had gathered along the quay and around the wide Place St Michel. Some were tourists, but most were curious onlookers discussing the morning's events. Local police were still patrolling, and the nearby cafes were enjoying the extra business the morning's events had brought to the wide square.

'No entry, monsieur,' a gendarme said to him.

'I live in Rue de la Huchette,' Alistair replied.

The gendarme nodded him through. Alistair walked slowly. He stopped at the kiosk and bought a crepe and coffee, his eye taking in the activity there. The square was a hive of people, police and that Gallic of all gestures, shrugs and up-raised hand movements. Keeping his head down, and sipping his coffee, he walked along the narrow street checking those around him. No one was paying him any attention. Everyone was totally absorbed in what the police were doing and telling anyone who'd listen what they remembered, truth or not.

Alistair pushed open the door and climbed the stairs. The door to number 7 was locked. 'Jenkins!' Alistair shouted, his boot hitting the door.

A few minutes later, he heard the lock rotate in its barrel.

'Why did you lock it? Who were you expecting, Interpol?'

Jenkins walked to the table and sat down. Alistair saw the inexpertly tied bandage wrapped around his upper arm. Some blood had seeped through. 'With a bloodied arm I can hardly go strolling around the streets. The police would be sure to detain me. And I'm fine, thank you for not asking.' Jenkins waited. 'Well?' He paused. 'You lost them, didn't you?'

'Yes, but not before I saw something unusual.' He told Jenkins about Irina and how the two men in the car had made their escape.

'And you didn't recognise either of the men from the car?'

'No. But one kept a helmet on, so I wouldn't know who that was. Interesting though, don't you think. Why would one be happy for passersby to see his face and the other not? A known or famous face, perhaps? But one thing's for certain; if Miss Goskova knew them, they are most likely Soviet.' Alistair drew in a deep breath and let out a long sigh then reached into his pocket for his cigarette case. He lit one and blew smoke into the air. 'But, with luck, I'll be able to learn who that was this evening.'

'How?'

Alistair sat down. 'I also received a message from Irina Goskova.'

'How?'

'You're beginning to sound like an actor from a spaghetti western movie, Jenkins.'

'Where then did you receive this message?'

'The bar in Place de la Madeleine.'

'How did she know you'd go there?'

'Maybe she double backed and was following me.'

'A bit far-fetched, even for you.'

'How would I know.'

Jenkins stared at the grimy window. 'You'll go?'

'Of course I'll go.' Alistair paused. 'I received another message from the barman in Place Madeliene. Apparently, Sir Giles wants me home.' Alistair explained the cryptic message about John Pevington.

'And Sir Giles is the only person who knew you had that alias?'

'Presumably. Although Miss McKillick may have as well. Don't see her as our undercover traitor, do you?.'

'No. Well, that's an end to your involvement here. We'll go home tomorrow together, and I'll have one of our doctors stitch my arm.'

'You must be joking! You can go home if you want to, but I wouldn't miss this for quids. Besides, I don't want to disappoint Miss Goskova.'

'My God! Is that all you think about? Don't answer that. You have one enormous ego.'

'It's not all I've got.'

Jenkins rolled his eyes.

'Have you spoken to Mother?'

'I rang as she requested. She said to stay here. She'd contact us.'

'Well, it better be before this evening, when I'm to meet Miss Goskova.'

'You're going out?'

'Don't take this personally but staying here in this dingy flat with you while Paris beckons seems like a waste of time to me.'

'You mother said she'd contact us. And if you're not here...'

'Just tell her I went out for coffee. I want to check the bar again. Jean knows more than he should.'

‘And Irina Goskova?’

‘I’m to meet her at nine at the *George V*.’

‘Bloody hell! Your mother’s going to kill us both. You for making rash decisions and me for letting you.’

CHAPTER EIGHTEEN

Paris

Sunday 21st July - Afternoon - Evening

Alistair stood at the window of the flat in Rue de la Huchette. Outside the slow twilight was descending. He checked his watch. Seven. He took the stairs to the street and walked to Place St Michel. He stood to one side of the large square, staring at the bridge ahead of him, the cars, bicycles, the motorcycles around him whizzing past. A nagging doubt lingered in his gut. Something about his nine o'clock rendezvous with Irina Goskova troubled him. He bit into his lower lip, wondering if he was walking into a trap. He lit a cigarette, speculating if he should have shared his doubts with Jenkins. But then Jenkins would only have told him not to go. And, regardless, Jenkins knew where he was going and who he was meeting. His thoughts returned to Irina Goskova. He imagined her lithe body, perfect skin and delicious fragrance. What was it about Irina? She seemed so guileless, innocent even. But why had she sent the message to meet? Surely it could only be to tell him something important. Perhaps she hadn't sent it at all but someone who wanted to entrap him? He crossed the square, heading for Pont St Michel. Whoever had left the message couldn't have known he'd ever return to the bar in Place de la Madeleine. Therefore, they couldn't have known if he'd ever receive the message. Was it just a chance invitation? One that didn't matter one way or the other if he received it. A letter in a bottle kind of request. Perhaps not only the British used Jean and his bar for clandestine acquisitions. He reached into his pocket for his cigarette case and, taking another out, lit it, the action automatic. He breathed in the strong tobacco. He hoped her message was only because she wanted to see him again. His thoughts dwelt on her smooth shape, her hips and breasts. He recalled the pompous art expert he'd interviewed in London. Gerard Martin-Something. How the man had gone on about curved lines and tactile smoothness. He'd clearly never seen the naked body of a beautiful woman. Although Alistair felt sure Martin-Whatever only saw naked women in works of art. He visualised Irina cradled in his arms and reflected on their intimacy. He'd enjoyed it more than he cared to admit and rather hoped she might be at the bar. But her motive in contacting him plagued him. He stopped short and stared over the bridge to the Seine below. Perhaps that wasn't quite the right question; it wasn't so much her motive in contacting him, but rather what was her motive in meeting him *again*? Attraction or entrapment?

'Only one way to find out,' he muttered to himself. Alistair flicked the cigarette butt into the river then crossed Ile de la Cité. He stared at his feet as he walked. That wasn't something he usually did. He preferred to look into the future in front of him; into the air that was filled with possibilities, sometimes fragrant and hopeful, sometimes not. So, what was it that vexed him about her message? He was meeting Irina Goskova, not Comrade Stalin. What could possibly go wrong?

Once across the Seine, he hailed a passing cab. 'Place de la Madeleine, merci.'

Alistair paid the fare, then crossed the square and walked towards the bar. Inside groups of people stood at the counter. While not as busy as a Saturday evening, it was moderately crowded. He checked his watch; just before eight. A burst of laughter came from a table in the far corner. People were doing what they always do in bars, drinking and enjoying themselves.

His eye scanned the room quickly, looking at the patrons, taking in the faces, especially anyone who looked out-of-place like a muscular flower seller. He also checked the women present. Dark-haired, elegant and sophisticated even if not beautiful, there was an aura about French women that exuded charm and allure, and was a perpetual attractant. 'You're like a moth to the flame,' he whispered to himself. But as seductive as these women were, Irina Goskova wasn't amongst them. He didn't expect her to be but everything about the alluring Russian made him question even himself. He felt the ambivalence. It was both disturbing and irresistible. The sensation was something he'd never felt before. He rather liked it. He sauntered up to the bar and caught Jean's eye.

'Whisky, monsieur?' Jean asked before Alistair could say anything.

'Oui, merci, Jean.'

The barman poured the single malt, and Alistair drunk it back whole. 'I see you did not take the Englishman's advice.'

Alistair placed the empty glass on the counter, and Jean refilled it. 'What do you know that I don't, Jean?' Alistair gambled.

'Ah, many things and nothing, monsieur.'

'Do you pass on messages for others who come in here? Others who perhaps are not English?'

'Perhaps.'

'And parcels?'

Jean caught his eye. 'Another word of advice, monsieur. Work out which advice should be followed and which ignored.'

'And how do I do that, Jean?'

The barman paused and held Alistair's gaze. 'Only a fool rushes to his death,' Jean said picking up the whisky bottle and tapping the cork back into the neck.

'I think...I think you may be right. But you haven't answered my question.' Alistair stared at the barman with different eyes.

'I haven't always been a barman.'

Alistair stared at the man, a thousand questions jostling for answers. The barman grinned then went to serve another customer. To Alistair he sounded like a professional operative. And perhaps he was. Or had been. Perhaps he'd worked for the Resistance during the war. Perhaps that was why he funneled parcels and information to Secret Service personnel of every nation. Or maybe he was just really good at keeping secrets. Then again, maybe the British Secret Service paid him better than most. But, if the barman knew more about Alistair's current situation, he wasn't saying.

Alistair caught the scent of her perfume and turned his head. He beamed at her. 'Jean, a bottle of the best champagne you have, thank you.' He turned slowly so his body was facing her. She was wearing her long cream trench coat and beneath it, he could see a black dress with a gold buckle at the waist and the highest pair of green and black stiletto heels he'd even seen. She looked edible. She joined him at the bar. He beamed and reached for her hand, kissing her fingers as she sat beside him. 'Champagne?'

'Are we celebrating?'

'Does one ever need a reason to drink champagne?'

She smiled.

'I thought the rendezvous was at the *George V* at nine?' he asked, pouring the champagne.

'Perhaps, like you, I wanted some, how do you say in English, Dutch courage.'

'You didn't need it last time.' He paused then lowered his voice. 'Why are you really here?'

'Why sit in a room waiting for time to pass, when I could be drinking champagne with a handsome man.'

'Now I know you're lying.'

She smiled. 'I played a hunch. I think we are much alike. But also very different.'

'So I repeat, my lovely, beguiling Irina, why are you here?'

'I want you to meet someone.'

Alistair's expression faded. His eyes flicked to the door. The tall, strong looking man with a full head of slicked-back, dark hair stood with his arms folded over his chest, baring the way. He had well-developed biceps visible through his shirt, a round face and thick set jaw. He was most definitely out of place in the bar amongst Paris's sophisticated set.

Alistair's hand reached into his coat, his fingers wrapping around the pistol.

Irina saw the movement. 'That won't be necessary. Besides, you don't want a scene. You really should have gone home, John Pevington.'

Alistair stared at her as his gut did a somersault. 'You once asked me who I was. Now, Irina, *you* have my full attention.'

'Not here. Too many eyes.'

'Maybe for you. For me, I prefer it. Were you following me?'

She leaned forward and kissed him on the mouth but didn't answer. She stood and walked towards the door, her perfume wafting over him. Alistair glanced at Jean then put a hundred US dollars on the counter for the champagne and the advice which Alistair wished he'd taken. He followed her to the door, his senses on high alert. Biceps-man at the door stepped aside, holding the door wide.

'Is he coming too?' Alistair asked.

'Yes. His name is Sergei.'

***

Ivkin ran towards the Soviet Embassy gate. He knew the cameras would have already seen him and the security guard would have alerted Boyanski. 'Let me in immediately!' he shouted at the guard. 'And notify Major Boyanski.'

The gate opened a fraction, and Ivkin ran through, heading for the side entrance. Boyanski was already there. 'Where have you been?' Boyanski asked looking past him. 'And where is Her Friedleman?'

'The British tried to kill us!' Ivkin said as Boyanski closed the door.

'Come to my office, Colonel. And please keep your voice down.' Boyanski led Ivkin along the back corridor to his office. Even though well after eight o'clock, there were still people working in the back corridors of the Soviet Embassy.

Boyanski closed the door and indicated for Ivkin to sit down.

'Could I have a vodka, Boyanski?'

'Of course, Colonel.' Boyanski went to the bar in his office and poured two drinks. He handed one to Ivkin then sat at his desk and swallowed his vodka whole. 'Now, tell me everything. And what is this about the British trying to kill you? I remind you, Colonel Ivkin that you were to telephone me the moment you got to the safe house. You didn't! You didn't even go to the safe house. I checked. So, I hope you have a good explanation for your behaviour. And where is Friedleman?'

Ivkin drank the vodka then leaned forward in the chair, his breathing exaggerated from running. He placed the glass on Boyanski's desk. 'Gone!'

'What do you mean, gone?' Boyanski shouted.

'We were going early for some breakfast. That was when it happened. A car sped into Place St Michel, screeched to a halt, and someone in a bulletproof car tried to assassinate Friedleman and very nearly killed me too. We hid, then after the car left, we ran for our lives. But as soon as we crossed the bridge, the British were waiting for us. I managed to escape, but they have Friedleman. We must get him back.'

Boyanski leaned over his desk. 'Dermo!' he stood and poured himself another vodka. 'Moscow Central Committee will be furious.'

'What? What are you talking about? What has Moscow Central got to do with this?'

Boyanski took a long breath. 'Colonel Ivkin. I received a telephone call from General Moshenko, of Moscow Central Committee. I was told that Friedleman was a traitor, and I was ordered to eliminate him.' Boyanski paused and stared at Ivkin. 'But perhaps this news isn't as much of a shock to you as it was to me.'

'Meaning?'

'You must have suspected Friedleman wished to defect, or you wouldn't have notified Moscow Central about the notebook.'

'Yes, I told them.' Ivkin pushed the empty glass across the desk, and Boyanski refilled it. 'Because I thought it dangerous to have the notebook in his home. It also occurred to me that he may try to defect. That was why Moscow Central allowed me to go with him at such short notice.'

'Have you seen this notebook?'

'No. If he has brought it, it must be concealed in the lining of his suitcase. He never lets it out of his sight, now I think about it.'

'We'll need to find him and carry out Moscow Central's order. They will not be happy that our first attempt didn't succeed. So it is mandatory that the second attempt is successful.'

'It was you in that black car!'

Boyanski nodded.

Ivkin slumped back into the chair before Boyanski's desk and drank the refilled vodka. 'This is unexpected news. We have to get Friedleman back before the British get him out of France.' He paused as though deep in thought.

'What should we do, Colonel Ivkin?' Boyanski asked.

'Let me think! Whatever we do, we must act carefully. This is very serious. For our country and for you personally, Boyanski. Failing to successfully carry out the orders of Moscow Central is serious enough, but couple this with your actions, that would be viewed as aiding the East German's defection,' Ivkin paused. 'Did you inform Moscow Central that Friedleman and I went to a safe house?'

'No.'

'Perhaps that is not the correct question. Did you inform anyone that Friedleman and I went into hiding?'

'Yes, Colonel Ivkin. I told my trusted source.'

'Was this trusted source with you in the black car?'

'Yes.'

'And it was he who attempted to kill us?'

'Not you, Colonel Ivkin. Just Friedleman.'

'Well, he very nearly killed me. Murder is a serious offense. But killing a KGB colonel without instructions would be seen not only as murder but also treason. Your source may be protected, but you won't be. Add this to a failure to carry out Moscow Central orders, and these misdemeanours will see you executed, Boyanski. And, from what I saw, your source is not a good shot. He missed. Happily for me, but not for you. And now, Friedleman is in British hands. What do you imagine will happen to you, when Moscow learns that Friedleman is living happily in the West. Not only sharing his secrets and latest inventions but that you have facilitated his defection to the West?'

'But I haven't?' Boyanski protested.

'When did you receive this order?'

'Yesterday.'

'And today, he disappears! Don't you think Moscow Central will put two and two together? Your actions confirm you aided his defection, especially after a bungled assassination attempt. You will be arrested, escorted back to Moscow where you will stand trial. And, it will be a very short trial. Then you will be shot.'

Boyanski sat motionless, his face becoming more pallid by the second.

'We must find him before the British remove him from France. Your source, are they inside the British Embassy here in Paris?'

Boyanski nodded. 'But he is very valuable where he is, and I cannot expose him. If we lost the information trail, it would be years before another such source could be found.'

Ivkin leaned back in the chair. 'You are a brave man, Boyanski to put your country's needs ahead of your own life. It will, however, not be a glorious death for you. But consider this; your contact will know where they have taken Friedleman. With his help, we may get him back. Trying to locate Friedleman in Paris any other way will take time. Time we don't have. Your contact can keep us informed of the British intentions.'

'I think he will assist. But I should go with him. My source's identity must remain secret.'

'No, Boyanski. It's too late for that. Besides, Friedleman wouldn't go with you willingly. I am the only one he trusts. It has to be me. Then once we are back here at the embassy, you can carry out Central Committee's order. And the French authorities will know nothing about it. Friedleman will be dead. Central Committee will be satisfied. And you will be alive.'

Boyanski licked his lower lip then bit it. 'Yes, I suppose you are right, Colonel Ivkin...'

'Of course I'm right. Do you care so little for our country to allow his inventions to fall into the hands of our enemy? Unthinkable! Not to mention your own limited future? And once he is on British soil, it will be exceedingly difficult for me to locate and remove him. It could take years for me to find him and carry out what you failed to do.'

Boyanski stood and walked towards his filing cabinets. Unlocking a drawer, he reached in for the recently developed photograph Ivan had taken of Boyanski's British contact making a telephone call from a public box in Les Invalides. Without speaking, he handed the photograph to Ivkin.

'Is this the man who attempted to kill Friedleman and myself earlier today in Place St Michel?'

'Yes.'

'How did you get away?'

Boyanski told Ivkin about Irina Goskova's bold initiative.

'And where is Miss Goskova now?'

'She left to find Friedleman and kill him and...'

'And?'

'Just an annoying young Englishman. My contact wanted him removed.

'Does this Englishman have a name?'

'Alistair Quinn.'

'Does this Alistair Quinn know about Herr Friedleman?'

'Yes. He was sent from England to locate Friedleman and learn what he could about him and his work.'

'And did he?'

'As far as I know, no.'

'So, he's a diversion. But why does your contact want him dead?'

'I don't know. Perhaps he is jealous, perhaps envious. Perhaps just spiteful. Or...'

'Or?'

'I think he liked Miss Goskova. More than liked. Perhaps the young Englishman had designs of his own for Miss Goskova. Jealousy is a powerful motive.' Boyanski shrugged. 'Either way, it soon won't matter.'

Ivkin's frown deepened. 'I don't care if our source wants to bed her or marry her. But this petty jealousy with a British Intelligence Officer, this Alistair Quinn, is inconvenient but of no consequence. And your contact acting in this manner is ridiculous. He could jeopardize everyone involved with this nonsense. Most unwise and unsafe. What is worth exposing and possibly sacrificing yourself for such a nobody. Ivkin stared at the photograph in his hand. 'It is important that this man's identity remains secret, even if he is a jealous moron. Who else knows about him?'

'No one.'

'Goskova? Does she know?'

'No. No one other than me knows. And now you.'

'How long has he been a contact?'

'Years. And always his information is high quality.'

'Then it is important that he remains in his current position.'

Boyanski nodded. 'What would you like me to do?'

'Stay here. I need you to remain by the telephone. If I or Goskova need assistance, we need you to be contactable and to arrange whatever assistance is required. Now I must hurry. Get me a car and driver. '

'Only the mechanic, Ivan Popovski is available. He can take you wherever you wish to go.' Boyanski lifted the telephone and dialled the number for the garage.

'A car will be at the side entrance in five minutes, Colonel Ivkin,' Boyanski said standing. 'Thank you.' Boyanski pulled himself up, his manner formal. He bowed at the waist.

'Colonel Ivkin, my future and my very life is in your hands,' Boyanski paused. 'I don't know how to repay you. I will forever be in your debt if you can find Herr Friedleman and bring him back here. How will you do this?'

'Better you do not know.'

'Anything I can do to help you, Colonel. Just call me. I will wait by the telephone all night, if I have to.'

Ivkin nodded then stood to leave. He turned to face Boyanski. 'It perhaps would be best not to inform your source of our plans. He is already doing a dangerous job. If the British suspected him, even for a moment, they would have him removed, and we need the intelligence he provides.'

'If you think it best, Colonel Ivkin.'

'I do. His identity must remain secret.' Ivkin left via the side entrance. As the car drove out of the Soviet Embassy's gate, Ivkin took the photograph from his pocket and studied the face.

CHAPTER NINETEEN

Paris

Sunday 21 July - Evening.

Once outside the bar, Alistair took Irina's arm and pulled her close to him. She'd pulled away as though repulsed by his touch. Over his shoulder, he felt the presence of the hulk named Sergei. 'Where are you taking me to have your wicked way with me?' he whispered into her ear.

'Somewhere safe,' she said, her tone flat and unemotional.

Sergei strode ahead of them. Alistair saw the well-built man standing beside a black car. He glanced at the tyres and metal wheel rims, but he knew it wasn't the same car he'd seen earlier in the day in Place St Michel. Sergei held the rear passenger door open. Irina walked to the opposite side of the car and opening the other rear door, sat behind the driver's seat.

Alistair watched her with a growing sense of unease. Gone was the provocative and naïve Irina; replaced by perfunctory procedure. Risk was always something he sought, but his gut feeling about Irina had him on high alert. And from what he had just seen, he was beginning to feel that he'd been played for a fool. He heard the barman's warning. *Only a fool rushes to his death.* Was Irina more than just a junior Soviet Official? Could she have been the assassin in the car? He knew she couldn't have been because of timing. He'd seen her on the motorbike, and the car hadn't stopped since leaving Place St Michel. He hoped that it was just Sergei's presence that was affecting her; a man who doubtless would report her every move to her superior. Alistair felt again for the pistol, its presence reassuring. He looked at Sergei. The Soviet driver was a big man, and from what Alistair could see of his hands and physique, he was considerably more powerful than himself. In fact, he believed those hands could squash the breath out of an elephant. Alistair sat in the rear, and the large man shut the door.

'Irina! What's going on?' he whispered in the few seconds he had before the driver took his seat behind the steering wheel.

'Nothing for you to worry about,' she said not making eye contact.

Alistair felt the icy chill. Her words did little to reassure him. Within seconds of Sergei sitting in the driver's seat, Alistair heard the sound of the door locks clicking into place. He looked across to Irina, but she didn't return his gaze, keeping her face turned towards the front. He felt his pulse rate quicken, his mind on high alert, but with the door locks in place, there was no chance of escape. The black Soviet car left Place de la Madeleine. From Rue Vignon, they merged onto Rue Tronchet heading towards the main east-west thoroughfare of Boulevard Haussman. Alistair studied the buildings and streets, memorizing locations, waiting for any opportunity to force the door or shoot the lock. At Boulevard Haussmann they turned right. In an instant, he knew they were not heading to the Soviet Embassy. A myriad of questions bubbled. But turning right meant only one thing; they were heading for the outskirts of Paris, if not leaving Paris itself.

Alistair watched from the windows as they crossed Place de la Republic. He glanced across at Irina. She seemed resolute, almost stern-faced. He reached for her hand which she quickly withdrew. He felt the frown cross his forehead. Suddenly she seemed like a complete stranger. And every bit the most professional intelligence officer he'd ever met. Calm. Resolved. No emotion. And totally in control. She reminded him of another stern-faced woman at least thirty years older. Irina, just like his mother, apparently had an agenda of her own. It amounted to total control. Appear amateurish, foolish even, and people will think you are either incompetent or inexperienced. In that moment he thought of another person whose level of control was extraordinary, his late father. It had only been after their mission to Finland that he'd begun to appreciate his father's professionalism. Frank Quinn planned ahead. Nothing left to chance. Alistair thought of his father's plan to capture the Russian KGB man, Vasali Vlatkov and his father's death in London. But that was almost three years ago. In his mind's eye, he could still see his father's dead body lying on the floor. And what for him now? He'd fallen for the honey trap. He would pay a high price for an evening of sexual pleasure. You really have to keep it in your trousers, he told himself. That is, if you get another chance at life, you idiot! He stared out the darkened windows. He was in Soviet control with no help, and no likelihood of help. He felt like a fool. Doubtless one rushing to his death. No one from MI5 even knew where he was. Jenkins would inform his mother of his rendezvous with Irina at the *George V* at nine. But a check of the hotel's surveillance cameras would show he'd never arrived. Regardless, by nine o'clock or soon after, he'd be dead. Or in the bowels of the Soviet Embassy being interrogated. In his mind he pictured the interrogation rooms at Leconfield House in London with their grey, windowless walls and furniture bolted to the floor. But Jenkins's recent descriptions of Soviet interrogation filled his head. Hours of brutal grilling at the hands of the hulk Sergei would be nothing like the interrogation Jenkins had put him through in Leconfield House where they'd first met and where he'd been recruited into MI5. Irina evidently had other ideas for his immediate future which didn't involve either sex or recruitment. But if murder was Irina's intention, why were they heading out of Paris? He stared at the back of the driver's head. 'Where are we going?'

'To a death.'

'Not mine, I hope.'

She didn't reply.

Alistair nodded. He pondered shooting them both now. But he could only shoot one before the other shot him. Or, he could take the risk and wait to see where Irina was taking him. He planned that when they got out of the car, he'd have a better chance of killing both. He wanted to ask her why. But he knew she wouldn't tell him. They sat in silence for some time. The twilight had descended, and although still only half past eight o'clock, Paris's nightlife was beginning to come alive. By midnight, the city would be buzzing with bright lights, music, dancing, shows, and all kinds of evening pursuits. He would be dead. Face down in the gutter. Just another homeless person for the French authorities to process. Alistair stared at the buildings, the last sights he'd ever see. Strange, he thought, when one ponders one's own death, it's always in a nice place surrounded by pretty scenery and loved ones. He felt the chortle rise from his throat. Who were they? For Alistair loved ones didn't exist. His father and sister were dead, and his mother...well, there he couldn't finish the sentence. He doubted she'd ever loved anyone. He also doubted she'd think twice about him, let alone miss him. Just the same as all who'd worked and died for the security services, once dead, forgotten. He'd have no funeral and no burial plot to mark that he'd ever lived. Just like his father. A lifetime of service that no one acknowledged.

The car drove through some tall gates into the darkness. The sign above the gate told him of his final resting place; The Cimetière du Père-Lachaise, one of the city's cemeteries. Alistair laughed aloud. He saw the driver's eyes shift to the rear vision mirror, and their eyes met. Perhaps this man thought him flippant or extraordinarily brave. But Alistair wondered if his laughter was not so much bravado but actual fear. Either way, he thought it ironic to be killed in a graveyard. 'Well, at least you won't have to carry me far.'

Irina didn't respond. Instead, she leaned forward and tapped the driver on the shoulder. 'Pull up here, Sergei,' she said in Russian. Alistair looked out of the window. Tombstones — some ancient and tall, some new and shiny — surrounded them on both sides. In the evening light, they resembled ghostly soldiers standing to attention in a field of weeds forever fertilized with the blood and bones of the dearly departed. From the corner of his eye he saw her pull a Makarov PM from the rear seat pocket. He felt his left eyebrow rise involuntarily no longer wondering why she had wanted to sit behind the driver. He saw it already had a silencer attached. He stared at her, his eyes wide and inhaled a long breath.

CHAPTER TWENTY

Paris

Sunday 21st July – Evening

Grace Quinn stood by the window of her apartment on the first floor in Rue Ste-Croix de la Bretonnerie and drew back the delicate blue silk curtain. The last of the twilight was fading, and streetlights made the city appear romantic. Light rain was falling. A floor below, she saw the car slow then reverse park into a small space on the footpath opposite. Two men got out.

Five minutes later, she heard the tap on the door. 'Go and let them in Jenkins.'

Jenkins did as instructed and opened the door. Ivkin and Ivan Popovski walked in. Jenkins turned to stare at Grace. 'Oh, my God!'

'Colonel Ivkin, Ivan, I trust everything went well?' Grace said.

Friedleman stood immediately. 'Ach du Lieber Gott!' Friedleman swore at Ivkin.

'Hopefully, one day, Kurt you will thank me,' Ivkin added.

'Jenkins, when you've finished gawking, you are to escort Herr Friedleman and Ivan Popovski to England.'

'And Colonel Ivkin?' Jenkins asked.

'No. There is a yellow Citroën parked downstairs. Drive to Calais but leave the car in the car park there, then take the ferry to England.' She reached into the desk drawer and withdrew a set of keys, then tossed them to Jenkins. 'You'll find passports for both men in the glove box. Once on board, throw the car keys into the Chanel.'

Friedleman was staring at Ivkin, his jaw clenched and his eyes wide and angry. He lunged forward, but Ivkin gripped his arm, turning it backwards.

'Himmel, Arsch und Zwirn!' Friedleman spat.

Ivkin gripped Friedleman's wrist and held it firm. 'There is no need for profanities. Besides, you will thank me, one day.'

Friedleman shook his arm free. 'Traitor!' He was almost shaking. 'They have a passport for me!' Friedleman hissed. 'All filled out, every detail about me, ready and waiting! Presumably with every detail! How could they do that without your instruction? So how long have you been planning my kidnap? Years! You disgust me!'

Ivkin didn't respond.

'As Colonel Ivkin says, Herr Friedleman, you will, in time, thank us for this,' Grace interjected. 'Now sit down and have a drink.' She turned to Jenkins. 'And Jenkins, not a word to anyone about what you've seen and heard here in Paris. Bill Trant will meet you on arrival at the Dover Terminal. Ivan Popovski you can trust. He works for us and is a willing defector. But stay close to Friedleman. He's still afraid and may try to escape. Although, given what the Soviets believe about him, perhaps not.'

Ivkin wandered over to the chair by the window and sat heavily. 'I have learned from Boyanski that the attempt on your life this morning Kurt was from Colonel Boyanski himself. He was ordered by Moscow Central Committee to assassinate you.'

'What! Why?' Friedleman squinted, his eyes filled with hatred. 'I don't believe you.'

'Regardless, it's true.'

'You betrayed me to them. It's about my notebook, isn't it? She has it! You used it to guarantee you'd come with me to

Paris where I would be branded a traitor by our own people. Now I cannot return to my home, because of you. And I will never see Marlis again.' Friedleman's eyes glazed. 'If she's still alive.' He paused. 'And, if she isn't, I'll kill you myself.'

'Enough of this!' Grace said. 'I've already told you Herr Friedleman that I will do everything I can to get your wife out. In fact, plans are already in place for it to happen. But you must leave now. There'll be time for recriminations in England.'

'My things! What about my suitcase? My notes for Monsieur Lebec?'

Grace stared at him. 'Your suitcase was collected this morning by our people, Herr Friedleman. As for Monsieur Lebec, you will have many happy years to make his acquaintance in future.'

'So you've thought of everything.'

'Thank you. I'll take that as a compliment.'

'What about Alistair?' Jenkins interjected. 'He went to meet Irina Goskova, I think at the *George V* Hotel.'

'Leave him to me.'

Jenkins didn't question his former boss. Besides, she wasn't a person to invite questions, especially from subordinates. And defying her directives would be met with more than an unfavourable response, the consequences of which didn't bear thinking about. He realised without doubt now that Grace Quinn had been orchestrating events all along, and while he now understood why he'd been ordered to Paris, he also understood that Alistair's presence had been a last-minute complication.

'What if I don't go with them? Friedleman said.

'Then we will hand you back to the Soviets. As you have already worked out for yourself, they will execute you for bringing secret documents to the West,' Grace snapped.

'Which I didn't. He did!' Friedleman said, pointing at Ivkin.

'They won't believe you.' Grace paused then lowered her voice. 'You are a dead man, Herr Friedleman, if you return.'

She held his gaze for a few seconds. Friedleman stared at her, his vitriolic expression gradually fading to indignant realisation as the circumstances of his position sunk in.

Friedleman turned to Ivkin. 'Are you going back to Berlin?'

Ivkin didn't reply.

'Please, if this woman can't get Marlis out, for all that we have shared in the past; I beg you, please look after Marlis. She is completely innocent.'

'I don't know where I'll be, Kurt, but I'll try,' Ivkin stood. 'You are leaving now. Go with these men. You will be in England by tonight.'

Jenkins reached for Ivkin's overcoat and held it while Friedleman put it on.

Ivkin turned to Ivan. 'Is the machine gun in the car?'

'Yes. The other car is still being repaired. I was ordered to empty the car and return the weapon to the gunroom at the embassy. I put it into the spare tyre cavity of the car downstairs.'

'And what did you do to it?' Ivkin asked.

'Who said I did anything?'

'No assassin misses that many times,' Ivkin added.

'Boyanski ordered me to get the weapon from the gun room. After I checked it out of the armory, I altered the sights by 15 degrees.'

'Which explains why you very nearly killed me and why Jenkins here took a bullet in the arm. Despite this, you did well. I'll dispose of it. Now give me the keys to the Soviet car.'

Jenkins stood beside the frightened East German scientist with Ivan Popovski on his other side. Wearing Ivkin's coat and hat, Friedleman along with Jenkins and Ivan left the apartment.

Grace stood by the window. Ten minutes later, she saw the yellow Citroën drive away. She walked over to a sideboard and poured two whiskies. 'Did Boyanski swallow it?'

'Oh yes. And we have the proof,' Ivkin said, pulling the photograph from his pocket along with a pistol which he put on the side table beside him. 'This is Boyanski's weapon, a Makarov PM, I took from his office. You'll need it to complete the deception.' Ivkin reached for the glass then sat again in the chair and took a few sips of the single malt whisky. 'Do you know, Boyanski ordered a photograph of me from KGB headquarters.'

'Really? Not quite so stupid then as I thought.'

'Stupid enough. I think, Grace that deception may be the masterstroke of your career. Substituting me for Vasali Vlatkov, KGB officer responsible for the death of a valued Estonian informant, and sending me to the USSR in a prisoner trade as him, was sheer genius. The Soviets never questioned that I wasn't Vlatkov. They assumed my aged appearance was due to captivity. They took my photograph and gave me a new name. How is our Russian?'

'Vlatkov?'

'Yes.'

'Angry. But then you would be too if you knew your countrymen had given up looking for you because they believed you'd been returned.'

'Now, only one thing remains.'

'Yes. Alistair.' Grace took a sip of her own drink, then walked over to the telephone and dialled the direct secure line for Bill Trant. It rang only twice.

'Grace? What news?'

'He's on his way. Jenkins and Popovski are with him. Bill, call Greaves. He is to go to the Cimetière du Père-Lachaise at midnight. And order him to have Julian Murray drive him there. No one else. And no one else is to accompany them or be told where they are going.'

'Right.'

Grace replaced the telephone receiver and turned to Ivkin. 'Do you think he is acting alone?'

Ivkin drained the glass. 'Not sure yet. Grace, I'll leave now,' Ivkin said, then reached into his jacket pocket for the keys to the black Soviet Embassy car parked in the street. 'If *Woodpecker* is to remain active, I must go.'

'Drive the Soviet car and park it somewhere well away from here. And, it may be best to remove the weapon.'

'I agree. I'll bury it with the Soviet driver.'

Grace smiled. 'And, when and if it is ever found, it will prove the Soviet's involvement in the debacle in Place St Michel.'

***

Ivkin drove the Soviet Embassy car to the Eiffel Tower and parked it in an adjacent car park amongst the cars hired by tourists. Standing between the parked cars, and using the belt from Friedleman's coat, he tied the weapon to his body, then pulled on the coat and fastened the buttons. He sauntered away from the famous structure and took a bus back into central Paris. Outside a nightclub on the Champs-Élysées, he took the Metro to the outskirts of Paris. Coming up into a light drizzle, he huddled into his coat, and walked towards the Cimetière du Père-Lachaise. As he entered the cemetery he saw a small *Fiat* car parked a little distance away in a side road. Ahead, he could hear voices. Removing his coat, he untied the weapon and laid the machine gun on the ground beside him. He stayed well back, hiding behind a large, winged-angel tombstone and watched.

***

'Unlock the doors, Sergei,' Irina said.

Alistair heard the locks release. He stared at Irina. He couldn't breathe. Then the thud like cough of the silenced pistol discharging. The driver, Sergei now lay slumped forward, his forehead resting on the steering wheel. The blood from the shot to the nape of his neck cascaded down the seat, turning his collar red until it flooded his shirt, oozing into his hair and clothing.

'Dear God!' he glared at Irina. 'I ask you again, Irina; who are you?'

'First, Alistair, I remind you that you were not meant to be here. You were told to stay in England. But you didn't. Then you were told to stay out of sight. Again you didn't. Then you were told to go home. This also, you disobeyed. None of the things you were ordered to do, you did. But at every turn, *Woodpecker* took advantage of your presence here because they are the consummate professional.'

'You are one of Mother's girls! Is that my mother's code name?'

'Yes, I work for your mother. However, I am not permitted to disclose *Woodpecker's* identity. All I will say is this, I have worked with and sometimes for *Woodpecker* for some time. And there is always a Plan B.'

'So what happens now? And what happens to this dead Soviet driver Sergei whatever-his-name-is?

'I thought I just said, there is always a Plan B.'

Alistair stared at her. An unfamiliar emotion gripped his throat. He felt the fear, the icy realisation coursed through him like a dagger, and he swallowed hard. But more than this, he felt utterly vulnerable. He searched her eyes for any sign that the recent arrival was expected. He saw only determination. Either way, he was a dead man. And if he needed any proof of her commitment, she had calmly killed the driver with a single shot to the back of his head using a silenced weapon. No emotion. With his pulse racing, he reached for the door handle and clicked it open. Drawing his coat around him against the rain, he stepped out and held his breath.

***

Ivkin's hand reached for his silenced pistol. About fifty yards in front of him, he could see a man and Goskova. The man was standing in front of Goskova, but her pistol was raised. From the surrounding darkness Ivkin heard a car door open. Out of the darkness, he saw Grace walking towards the stationary car. Lifting his pistol, he fired one shot into the air as the sound of tyres crunched the gravel. He turned and watched as a car approached, its headlights lighting the scene ahead. In the glare of the lights, he could see the tall young man he'd seen outside the Soviet Embassy. Ivkin watched as two men alighted from the car and walked towards the group.

He recognised them both. With a clear line of sight, he silently stood and took aim.

***

Alistair saw the stream of light. He turned. Through the increasingly heavy rain he saw a vehicle pull up behind them, the headlights penetrating the dark night, exposing both himself and Irina. 'Is this part of your plan? Do you know who has just arrived?'

Irina turned to stare at the car. Alistair followed her gaze. But with the glare of the headlights and the rain, he couldn't tell who'd arrived. He stood motionless. On the night air, he heard the distinctive sound of the safety catch being loosed. Throwing himself to the ground he rolled over and over out of the glare from the headlights and into the mud and surrounding weeds. In the darkness all he could see were the headlights of the car behind. He stood and squinted into the glare, standing in a pool of water and light, waiting to be killed. The car's engine was turned off, and two car doors opened. Then two sets of legs, backlit by the headlights walked towards him. He could hear his own exaggerated breathing. But there was no pain. Nothing. If a bullet had been fired it had missed. or been intended for someone else. But if not him, then who? He didn't move. Fear was paralysing him. If ever he'd wanted

Jenkins, it was now. He'd seen two sets of men's legs arrive. Who were they? And what of Irina Goskova? She was a complete enigma; neither trusted nor hated. Neither Despise Nor Fear. His family motto came to him, and he realised the absolute truth of it for anyone who led a secret life. Emotion gets you killed. His father's words. Think! he silently shouted.

'What the hell is happening here?' It was Sir Richard Greaves's voice.

'Stand away from the car, Sir Richard!' Irina said. 'Alistair! Come here!'

Alistair stood still out of the rim of light. He tried to think, but there was so little time. He needed to make a decision quickly. Surely if she'd intended to kill him, she would have done so by now and he'd be dead alongside the Soviet driver. But why was Sir Richard here? And who was the other man? He waited out of the piercing shafts of light.

Irina stood to his right. He could see she was holding a pistol in her grip, and it was pointed at Sir Richard and the other man. Alistair saw him now. The second man was Julian Murray, the arrogant Legal Attaché from the British Embassy. But why were the British Cultural Attaché and the embassy's Legal Attaché in a Paris City cemetery? Alistair stepped forward.

'What is the meaning of this?' Sir Richard was demanding. 'And what is he doing here?' Sir Richard said pointing at Alistair.

'Don't move, any of you,' Irina said.

Alistair watched, both men and Irina had his full attention. Was he superfluous to need or there as a witness to the bizarre events unfolding? His gaze shifted between Sir Richard and Murray. Irina kept the pistol levelled on both men. If either or both of them were armed, neither moved.

'Are we to wait all night?' Sir Richard demanded.

'No. Just till my companions arrive,' Irina said.

'And him?' Murray said pointing at Alistair.

'I don't...' Alistair began.

In that instant, Murray backed up to the *Jaguar* car behind and kicked at the headlight with the heel of his boot, the glass shattering, the light of the other headlight now only illuminating Sir Richard and Alistair. Murray ran backwards into the darkness and away from the piercing shafts of light from the remaining headlight. Alistair pulled his L9A1 from his pocket, holding it with both hands. But in the gloom, he couldn't see where Murray had gone. With his eyes wide, he watched Sir Richard and Irina, but neither moved. Had Murray gone for help? Then the sound of footsteps on gravel. Behind him.

Someone lunged at Alistair from the darkness, and he felt the full weight of a man tackle him to the ground. He fell backwards, the man's body pinning him down. In the sudden onslaught, Alistair dropped his pistol and struggled with his assailant. He knew in a second it was Murray although why Murray should want him dead eluded him. Murray was strong. Stronger than Alistair had believed. He was on top of him now, the strong arms pinning his arms down, his head over him, a grin on his face. Then on the night air another distinctive burst of air was fired. Murray's full weight fell on him, his body limp and his blood soaking into Alistair's clothes. The shot had come out of the night. Accurate and deadly. Alistair pulled himself out from under the dead body of Julian Murray. He rolled over and stood, his coat was covered in mud and congealing blood. Murray's face was frozen in time. Irreversible, unmoving death had overcome him in an instant. Out of the gloom, Alistair saw the familiar legs, the almost nonchalant stroll. His mother, Grace Quinn walked towards the small group, a pistol in her hand. Alistair turned around. The body of Julian Murray lay in the dirt.

'Alistair, give me the passport for John Pevington,' Grace said.

He stared at the people close to him, Irina and Sir Richard. While Irina's expression remained resolute, Sir Richard showed shock and incomprehension. He stood motionless in the light, staring at the dead body of his colleague, Julian Murray. Alistair watched his mother. Although he had many questions, he didn't speak. Reaching into his coat pocket he withdrew the passport of John Peveington and handed it to her. Whatever was happening, the former Director General of MI5, Dame Grace Quinn was in complete control.

'There is some vacant land to the left of where the Soviet car is parked,' Grace told him. 'Dig a grave then put the body of the Soviet driver in it, then fill it in.' She walked over to where Murray lay and, taking the Makarov from her coat pocket, she bent down and fired one shot at point blank range into the base of Murray's neck, then stood. When you've finished with the Soviet driver, put Murray behind the steering wheel. Put the Makarov on the seat beside him and the passport for John Pevington in his upper shirt pocket. The French Police will take care of him tomorrow when he's found.'

'Grace? What on earth is happening here? And why are you in Paris?' Sir Richard said.

'A traitor has been unveiled and an awkward situation dealt with, especially for you. He's suffered a traitor's death, and difficult questions about him, which you would have to answer, can be avoided when he's found in a Soviet Car. You must be prepared, however, Sir Richard to be questioned by our own people and perhaps the French Secret Service. Harbouring a Soviet spy and giving him access to secret documents would be seen as aiding his treason.'

'What? Are you sure? I know nothing about this.'

'So, incompetence or collusion?'

'Neither! I'm astounded! Murray was...'

'One of us? Yes, one of us has always been a problem. Never forget Philby who was also one of us! Besides, I have proof of his guilt.'

'My god! How long has he worked for them?'

'Years! It's taken me and someone who is in deep cover many years to unearth the leak.' Grace turned to face Irina. 'You've done well, Irina.' Grace drew a handkerchief from her pocket and wiped the Makarov pistol she'd used to shoot Murray. She then grasped the barrel with the handkerchief and handed the weapon now wrapped in the cloth to Alistair.

'Whose pistol?' Alistair asked.

'Major Boyanski's Makarov will be discovered by the French police tomorrow. Then Boyanski will either be extradited back to the Soviet Union or imprisoned here on murder charges.'

'Is Irina coming with us?' Alistair asked.

'Us? Why would you assume you'll be coming with us? You have been a considerable nuisance, Alistair! And completely solipsistic! You will bury the Russian. You will place Murray behind the steering wheel of the Soviet car and make sure the Makarov is on the seat beside him and the passport in his top pocket then make you own way back to the British Embassy to report in with Sir Richard that you have carried out these instructions. And this must all be done before dawn. Understood! After that, you will return to the flat in Rue de la Huchette where you will stay until you get a signal from me to return to England as Simon Cordery. Once home, come and see me at Century House.' She turned to face Irina. 'You'll leave Paris tomorrow morning. Could you get the shovel and pick from the boot of my car? Give them to Alistair. He'll need them. Then wait for me in the *Fiat*. I'll drive us back to Paris.'

Irina did as instructed and returned within minutes. Alistair took the wide-bladed shovel and pick from her. He glanced at his mother then back to Irina. 'How long have you worked for my mother?'

'Not you concern,' Grace said.

'Irina said she worked for *Woodpecker*. Is that you, Mother? Are you *Woodpecker*?'

'In fact, *Woodpecker* is two specific people of whom I am one.'

'Then would you answer me one thing?' Alistair pointed off to his left. He knew the silenced shot he'd heard earlier had come from somewhere beyond them, about thirty yards away and in a different direction from where his mother had joined the group. Someone waited there, and he really wanted to know who. 'I heard a shot out there in the darkness. From a silenced weapon. As if it was a signal. Then another shot, the one that killed Murray. So now I ask, who shot Murray? You shot Murray in the head, we all witnessed that, but he was already dead. Killed by an assassin who doesn't miss. And who is possibly still out there.'

'Again, not your concern,' Grace said.

'I assume then if *Woodpecker* isn't Irina and you, then either he or she is hereabouts. Am I right?'

'Do as you're told, Alistair. And who fired the fatal shot, isn't your concern. Now, you have work to do.'

Alistair watched them walk away. He held the pick and shovel. Not knowing if the real killer was still in the cemetery was unnerving. It had him on edge. The cemetery was quiet now. Too quiet. He felt the unknown presence lingering, and it made his skin crawl. He grabbed the shovel and walked towards the Soviet car and found the bare ground beside it. Hanging his wet coat over a nearby tombstone, he rolled up his sleeves then swung the pick, his thoughts on recent events. He guessed Sir Giles sending him to Paris had caused his mother to alter her plans, and his presence had made many things difficult. And digging a deep hole in the rain was her revenge. It wasn't his fault, and he would remind her of that. Later. Not now. But even though he'd incurred her ire, he found himself in awe of her. She always had a Plan B. He'd watched his mother and Irina leave in the *Fiat*. Neither woman had looked back at him or anyone. As the rain trickled down his face, his thoughts returned to his mother, the women who'd given him life: cold, hard, remote and definitely ruthless. Perhaps, existence was all she'd ever given him. As much as he felt like walking away from the onerous task she'd given him, he didn't dare. Not because he feared his mother, which he probably did, but because the deception she and *Woodpecker* had so thoroughly planned depended on it. He felt himself shivering. He knew he was drenched and by morning's light would, most likely, catch a cold but at least his coat, although sodden, would not be caked in mud. He stared at the dark, wet earth with only the moonlight to see by. Having never dug a grave before, he cut a line into the dirt about four feet wide and seven feet long with the shovel, hoping it was long enough for the Soviet driver. Then he grasped the pick and swung it deep into the dark earth. At least, with the inclement weather, the dirt was soft. But the rain created another problem; the exposed dirt quickly became mud, and he found himself standing in slush. With each swing of the pick, the sides caved in filling the watery pit. He swore to himself, shoveling the mud off to his right. 'Fuck it! This is going to take hours!' he swore under his breath. He wondered why he'd whispered in the deserted graveyard. It was definitely not his idea of a pleasant way to spend the small hours of a foul night. He thought of Irina, of her warm body and delectable skin and lips. But the lovely Irina had two sides, and while one was soft and warm and delicious, the other was capable of cold-blooded murder. And this had made him feel amateurish. No, he thought, swinging the pick into the soil and shoveling it to one side, that wasn't fair. Irina, like his mother, was a professional. He'd made himself look foolish. 'Just keep it in your pants, your idiot!' he swore aloud. The barman's words about rushing to one's death refused to be ignored.

***

Ivkin watched the drama unfold. He saw Sir Richard drive himself away in his black *Jaguar*. The two women left in the *Fiat*. He watched as alone now in the cemetery, Alistair picked up the pickaxe and shovel and walk towards an area to the side of the Soviet car. Ivkin estimated it would take Alistair several hours of hard manual work to dig the grave and switch the bodies then replace the soil. And, it was already after midnight. Secreting the machine gun beside a grave away from the main path and with the young Englishman occupied for several hours, Ivkin slipped away from the cemetery. Half an hour later, he took the stairs to the Metro that headed back into Paris.

***

Grace and Irina drove back to the city. The rain was increasing. 'You've done well. But you cannot return now, Irina. I will find you something else. But first, you should have a holiday. Anywhere you like.'

Irina stared through the front windscreen as the wipers hurled themselves back and forth over the windscreen. The tiny *Fiat* sped along the wet Paris streets. She thought about Alistair shoveling the sodden earth, a slight smile on her lips. She wouldn't mind seeing him again. 'Tahiti, perhaps? I hear the beaches are beautiful and the water warm. All year round.'

'And who told you that, I wonder,' Grace added.

***

Just on two o'clock, Ivkin pressed the intercom button beside the enormous, closed green doors of the British Embassy that faced Rue du Faubourg St Honoré. A voice answered.

'Could you tell Sir Richard that Colonel Grigori Ivkin wishes to speak to him.'

'Could you repeat your name please, Sir?'

'Colonel Ivkin.'

'One moment, Sir. I'll see if Sir Richard is available to see you.'

Ivkin smiled visualising the chaos his arrival at the gate of the British Embassy was causing within the elaborate corridors. 'Perhaps you should look for him in the Legal Attaché's office,' Ivkin said into the intercom and reaching for his cigarette case. He huddled into his coat and leaned against the high stone wall while he waited. Moments later, the large green doors opened, and Ivkin stepped into the wide paved front courtyard. He saw the *Jaguar* parked there. Greaves hadn't even waited to park the vehicle in the secure underground car park, such was his hurry to find Murray's treachery. He imagined the Cultural Attaché combing through all Murray's correspondence of the last year searching for evidence of his betrayal. Ivkin glanced at the camera positioned high on the inner wall, but he imagined his arrival was secondary to the turmoil going on inside. The door opened. A man stood before him, a man he didn't know. And a man who wore a most suspicious expression.

'May I assume from the hour at our gate that you are requesting asylum, Colonel Ivkin?' the man asked.

Ivkin heard the footsteps. Sir Richard walked into the entry foyer and stood staring at them. 'Good Lord! Thank you, Cummins, that will be all.'

Ivkin stepped inside into the foyer and removed his wet coat. 'I need to ask a favour. Can we talk?'

Greaves took the coat and tossed it over the stair balustrade. 'Of course. I'm assuming you're involved and know about this night's events?'

'Yes. And I wouldn't mind a whisky right now,' Ivkin said. 'Perhaps your man could hang my coat somewhere where it will dry?'

'I'll see to it. I think we could both do with a drink.' Sir Richard led him into the drawing room at the rear. He closed the door to the foyer and switched on the light. The curtains were already drawn, but the house was far from silent. Ivkin imagined Greaves had everyone employed there already going through Murray's office. Greaves walked over to a phone and dialled three numbers. 'Cummins, Colonel Ivkin's coat is in the foyer. Could you see to it?' He replaced the receiver.

'I imagine you have been in Murray's office since you returned?'

'Yes. We'll find the evidence, even if it takes weeks.' Greaves poured two whiskies and handed one to Ivkin. 'Does Grace know?'

'Of course. It was she who suspected the leak was in Paris. But we also wanted Friedleman. He's been working on over-the-horizon radar and had worked for the Nazi's at Peenemunde during the war. A scientist we wanted. Grace saw a way of achieving two results in one operation. We've been working on the logistics of this for some time. We had everything in place just waiting for the catalyst.'

'And what was that?'

'A notebook. Actually, I didn't think it would succeed, but it appears it has, even with Sir Gile's unexpected involvement.' Ivkin paused and sipped his whisky. 'Did you have any inkling about Murray?'

'None whatever...' Greaves lowered the glass from his lips, his face falling. 'I hope Bill doesn't suspect me of any collusion?'

'MI6 suspects everyone, you know that. But it has put a cloud over your position here. I suspect you may lose this post. A word of advice, if I may. Don't take it personally. And maybe take early retirement. But, if you do continue in the diplomatic service, perhaps, in future, not so many parties.'

Greaves nodded then swallowed the remainder of his whisky. 'I won't sleep a wink for a month. I never suspected Murray, you know. A little brusque at times but a good chap. Or so I thought.'

'One of us?'

Greaves stood and walked over to the drinks cabinet in the corner. 'Yes, one of us. A phrase Grace used to me this night. It's a salient reminder that we have to be on alert at all times. No one is above suspicion. Of course, I know this. But it is amazing how one can become complacent. You just don't think it can happen on your watch. Especially in Paris. Berlin of course, everyone is tense there but Paris! Silly of me, of course. Will you have another?'

'No, thank you.'

'Mind if I do?'

Ivkin shrugged. 'Your whisky.'

'I suppose I'll be relieved. Good thing Muriel is in England. She'd only ask awkward questions. She'll miss the shopping here, I suppose.'

'How is your wife?' Ivkin asked.

'Homesick, actually. Is it likely they'll send me on gardening leave?'

'Perhaps. However, some details remain. And I have a favour to ask.'

CHAPTER TWENTY-ONE

Paris

Monday 22nd July 1968 - Early Morning

'How could I refuse?'

'I want you to engage Alistair as the Legal Attaché here. Just for twenty-four hours or so. Starting tomorrow.'

Greaves lowered his whisky glass, a deep frown settling on his forehead. 'Are you joking? He's not the most discreet person I've ever met. Neither, I imagine, would he take orders easily. Does he have any legal knowledge?'

'None that I know of. But he does speak Russian. He'll need supervision, of course, but it must appear as though Murray is still at his post. It's only for a short time; until the Soviets learn that Boyanski has been taken into custody. Alistair is quite a good mimic. Everything should be passed by you of course, but if things don't go as planned, and Boyanski attempts to make contact, I want someone convincing on standby to receive any messages. And to inform us of this contact.'

'How will you get Boyanski?'

'Better you don't know.'

'Is that likely Boyanski will make contact? Should I have Bill Trant send someone over?'

'No, I don't think that's necessary. Boyanski will be held in custody by the French Police. Of course, the Soviet Ambassador will be informed. But it never hurts to be prepared.'

'Of course. How do I reach you?'

'Through Grace. I'll give you the number.'

'Right!' Greaves chortled. He sat down and took a long sip of the whisky. 'I almost feel sorry for Boyanski. If he's caught in one of Grace's traps, he'll not know what's got him till it's all over. And perhaps not even then. Where is Alistair at present?'

'He'll be here soon. Grace told him to report in to you after he'd buried the Soviet driver and placed Murray behind the steering wheel of the Soviet car. If for any reason, he didn't show up here, Grace will know how to locate him.'

'What are you going to do now?'

'Again better you don't know.' Ivkin stood. He needed to leave with enough time to set the trap for the last remaining piece of the puzzle. 'I'll take the back way out. Perhaps you can offer the Legal Attaché post to Alistair when he arrives here later to report in. Don't let him have too much information. He's not a risk. He's just unpredictable. Then when Grace calls you, send him home. He'll be knocking on your door soon, so I should leave.'

Wishing him well, Greaves walked with Ivkin to the lift which would take him to the garage and the side street beyond. Grigori Ivkin disappeared into the darkness. As he left the British Embassy, he checked his watch. Not quite three o'clock. Outside he walked towards the Champs-Élysées and hailed a passing cab.

Twenty minutes later, he ran up to the Soviet Embassy gate and pounded on the guard's window. 'I'm Colonel Ivkin. Telephone Major Boyanski immediately.'

'Sir, it's almost three o'clock in the morning!'

'I don't care what time it is. Call him! And that's an order.'

The startled guard lifted the telephone receiver. It was a short conversation. 'He'll meet you at the side entrance, Colonel.'

Ivkin rushed through the gate and strode to the side of the monolith. Boyanski stood in his dressing gown by the door. 'Colonel Ivkin! What news?'

'I followed a car that left the British Embassy to The Cimetière du Père-Lachaise. I saw everything. But we should not have this conversation here.'

Boyanski stood back and allowed Ivkin to enter. They walked in silence along the deserted corridor to Boyanski's office. Boyanski unlocked the door. 'Tell me all.'

'The British definitely have Friedleman.'

Boyanski's eyes widened. 'Is he dead?'

'I don't know, but I wouldn't think so. He's too valuable. I know who has been informing the British about our every move. Boyanski, you can redeem yourself from that failed assassination attempt by helping me now to apprehend a real traitor. Someone who has been feeding all our information to the British. But we must be careful. When they first took me and Friedleman from Place St Michel to an apartment on the Right Bank, I overheard them plotting how they were going to lure your source, Julian Murray to a meeting. It was to The Cimetière du Père-Lachaise. But, now that I have escaped again, they will be looking for me. Someone will be watching the Soviet Embassy. They may have even seen me enter here just now, so they will assume I'll lie low here where they cannot touch me. But they will be ready to intercept me the moment I step foot outside this building. If we are to catch the traitor and rescue Friedleman, we must go to this meeting in the cemetery then inform the French Police. But we should leave here separately and travel separately.'

'What of Julian Murray?'

'He's dead. I saw him killed.'

Boyanski stiffened, his mouth fixed hard. 'Who betrayed us?'

'Irina Goskova.'

'I don't believe it!'

'Really? Did you tell her about your orders to assassinate Friedleman?'

'Yes. You had already vanished along with Friedleman. She said she'd find you. I told her to look around the Latin Quarter. Then she telephoned me to say you were in a street in the Latin Quarter; Rue Garancière. But surely that only proves her loyalty.'

'Then answer me this; why did she stay around Place St Michel and why was she there at six o'clock the next morning? Did you inform her of the details of your plans to assassinate Friedleman?'

'No...'

'So tell me this then; if she had located us and telephoned you with the address why didn't she return to the embassy? Unless she already knew something was going to happen in Place St Michel and when. And, how did she know to be on a motorcycle that just happened to be there for you and Murray to escape unless she had been in Place St Michel and seen the black Soviet bulletproof car? A car she recognised!'

'Dermo!' Boyanski swore. He ran his hand over his mouth and chin, his head shaking in disbelief. 'But surely this again proves her loyalty?'

'She has played us both expertly. Mixing lies with truth. But half-truths are still lies, disguised lies but lies nonetheless.'

'Colonel Ivkin. Again, I am in your debt. We must get her and find out what she's told them.'

'And before she has a chance to defect.'

'Dermo!'

'Yes. But we need to be careful. I'll wait here for you to change your clothes.'

'I won't be long.' Boyanski rushed away.

Ivkin heard him run along the corridor and climb the stairs. Closing the door to the corridor, he went straight to the cupboard. Hanging beside two overcoats, Ivkin retrieved the large bulletproof vest. Removing his jacket and jumper, he pulled the vest over his head, then replaced the jumper and jacket, smoothing down the padding.

Boyanski returned in ten minutes. 'How will we do this, Colonel Ivkin?'

'They are going to meet someone, I suspect a driver, who will take Goskova and Friedleman away in a car. They are to meet in The Cimetière de Père-Lachaise at four o'clock this morning.'

'Why there?'

'Because at that hour it will be deserted. And, as it is on the outskirts of Paris they can get away to the coast quickly and unimpeded.' Ivkin looked at his watch. 'Now we must leave! It will take us about forty minutes to get there. Do not take the same taxi from here to there. Switch vehicles at least three times. And Boyanski, be on your guard. You leave here first. I'll wait a further ten minutes.'

'I won't let you down, Colonel Ivkin. You are a very brave man. I would like to ask you about your escape.'

'It can wait until we are safely back here with Goskova and Friedleman.'

Boyanski shook Ivkin's hand, and they parted. Ivkin watched Boyanski leave the building. Ten minutes later, Ivkin left. About a hundred yards away from the Soviet Embassy, Ivkin hailed a cab on Boulevard Lannes.

The rain had abated. Ivkin walked through the cemetery gates. 03:35. He wanted to be early to make sure everything was as it should be. Ahead he could see the black Soviet car where Murray lay slumped over the steering wheel. Glancing around him, he checked he was alone. Alistair was nowhere to be seen. With his hand on his pistol, Ivkin approached the car. Standing beside it, he peered in. Murray was still there. A large amount of blood had congealed around his neck had dripped onto his lap. Boyanski's Makarov pistol lay beside him. In the ghostly pre-dawn light, Ivkin walked the short distance to where he knew the body of Sergei the Soviet driver lay buried. The soil looked fresh. Checking over his shoulder to make sure he was unobserved, he returned to where he'd hidden the Russian machine gun. He carried it back to where Sergei lay buried and kicking at the loose soil, he uncovered a few inches, then laid the weapon in the small ditch. Using his foot, he covered the weapon then stamped his feet over the loose soil, packing it down. From a nearby path, he scattered some gravel over the site. He stood back. The weapon was only just concealed and would easily be found with a heavy downpour of rain. Checking the surrounding graves, he saw a bunch of flowers in a brass urn. He walked towards it and removed some pink roses from the vase. 'Fitting!' he muttered remembering the flowers he'd given to Grace on the bridge. He then laid the flowers on the compacted soil and stood back. On the crisp air he heard the sounds of several cars driving on gravel and coming from the main gate into the cemetery. He checked his watch. 03:50. They headed away from where he was standing. He saw them disappear behind a long hedge. The thick silence returned.

At exactly four, he saw Boyanski walking towards him. The man wore a heavy coat and hat. Ivkin thought too heavy. He wasn't expecting trouble, but he felt for his own pistol, its presence reassuring.

'Boyanski. There is a dead man here. Is this your contact? Ivkin asked, pointing towards the car.

Boyanski rushed towards the car and looked inside. 'Dermo! That's him. And Goskova?'

Ivkin shook his head.

'What is going on, Colonel?' Boyanski asked.

Ivkin shrugged. The blaring sound of a siren broke into the still air. A car came at speed towards them, its headlights illuminating everything around them. Stopping on the gravel, it blocked the main road out of the cemetery. Parked a little further back were another two police vehicles. Several men, wearing dark clothes and four gendarmes got out.

'Stay where you are! Hand on your heads! Don't move!' a man wearing a long trench coat and hat said as he walked towards them, his body backlit from the car's harsh headlights. He held his handgun high and pointed at them.

Four gendarmes surrounded Boyanski and Ivkin. Two other men stood nearby, and a further plain-clothed man joined them.

One gendarme walked to the Soviet car and looked inside . 'There is a dead man here, Inspector. Shot from behind!'

The Inspector kept his eyes on Boyanski and Ivkin. 'You are both under arrest.'

'I have nothing to do with this!' Boyanski protested. 'I am a Soviet diplomat, and you cannot arrest me! Colonel Ivkin is also a Soviet citizen and diplomat. We have immunity!'

'Save it for the judge!' the Inspector calmly added.

'There is a pistol here, Sir,' the gendarme called.

Ivkin and Boyanski were led towards the two parked cars, a gendarme on both sides of them. About ten yards from the parked police vehicles, Ivkin lunged sideways, throwing himself into the nearby grass and rolling over. He quickly stood then in one quick move, he threw himself towards a nearby headstone. The gendarmes reacted immediately. Pulling their pistols from their belts, they fired their weapons hitting Ivkin in the chest. Ivkin was thrown backwards, several bullets hitting him. His body lay motionless beside a low, flat grave.

'Colonel Ivkin!' Boyanski shouted.

'Get him out of here!' shouted the inspector.

Boyanski was pushed towards the first car. 'You've killed a Soviet citizen! My country will be outraged about this.'

'Should I telephone the City Mortuary and have this man's body collected, Sir?' one gendarme asked the inspector.

'No. I will take care of this man. You take Comrade Boyanski to the City Police Station and put him in a maximum security cell until I give orders otherwise.'

'This is an outrage!' Boyanski was protesting. 'I have nothing to do with this!' The rear door of the police car was slammed shut. Within minutes, it drove away.

Grace watched from the second police car as the car carrying Boyanski disappeared from the cemetery. Opening the car door, she stepped out. 'He's gone!'

Grigori Ivkin stood and walked towards the remaining police car. 'Three shots, Inspector? I'll be bruised for weeks. But our friend Boyanski is a witness to my death.'

The inspector smiled. 'I think he was convinced.'

'I thought so too,' Grace said. 'So, *Woodpecker*, will you come in now?'

'Most probably but perhaps not till Frau Friedleman is in Britain...'

'Until you decide, you can use the apartment in Rue Ste-Croix de la Bretonnerie. Do you have a passport with you?'

Ivkin nodded.

'And some money?'

'Yes. If I need anything, I'll contact you through our barman friend.'

The inspector opened the driver's door and sat inside. 'So Boyanski thinks he has been arrested by us for killing a man he says he doesn't know but who is a British citizen named John Pevington.'

Grace turned to him. 'Inspector, Boyanski, of course, does recognise the body as that of Julian Murray, but he isn't likely to tell you or anyone that. Although he will find it difficult to explain how his pistol was found in the car beside Murray's body. Such evidence will see him charged with murder. It would also implicate him in espionage on French soil. And, diplomat or not, it would see him returned to the Soviets where I imagine he wouldn't receive a hero's welcome given all that's happened. The Soviet Ambassador will have to be informed, but Boyanski could be offered a way out.'

'I'm not sure I can get him extradited, madame, if that is what you're thinking,' the Inspector added.

'Oh, I think between us we can arrange that. I'm sure your government will be only too happy to see the back of a man like Boyanski. They have no liking for foreign nationals who attempt assassinations in the streets of Paris and kidnap unsuspecting tourists, like poor Mr Pevington, in a Soviet bulletproof car only to be gunned down in cemeteries in the middle of the night,' Grace said. 'If Boyanski pleads guilty to the murder of John Pevington, a British citizen, and you extradite Boyanski to Britain, he'll be tried for murder. If he protests; we'll hand him back to the Soviets and inform them how he shot Julian Murray, a valued Soviet mole in MI6 and arranged the defection of his subordinate, an experienced female intelligence officer. I'm sure they'll eventually either hang him or send him to the icy wastes of Northern Russia to work in the gulags. Given the choices, he'll choose a comfy jail cell in Britain. The world's press will show some interest in him for a while but then, as they always do, they'll forget about him. So, in the end, France doesn't have to deal with an international incident, The West has a valuable scientist, a

British traitor is quietly removed, a KGB agent implicated in murder and espionage is removed from his post, and a scandal on French soil averted. A thoroughly successful outcome.'

'They'll want him back,' the inspector said.

'And they'll get him! In exchange of Frau Friedleman. But that will happen when we're ready.'

'Why would you do that?' the inspector asked.

'To fulfill a promise I made,' Ivkin interrupted. 'He'll be traded for Frau Friedleman. And Grigori Ivkin is dead. Boyanski, himself, was the witness.'

Two police cars sped across Paris. No sirens were blaring. Just before 0600, one car entered the basement car park of the Paris City Police station. There the hand-cuffed Boyanski was taken inside. At the same time in Rue du Faubourg St Honoré, the other French police car drove into the underground car park under the British Embassy.

Grace and Ivkin got out of the car. 'Thank you, Inspector. I'll be in touch in the next few days.'

'Always a pleasure Madame Quinn. Monsieur. Au revoir.'

'A bientôt, Inspector.' Grace opened the rear door into the British Embassy. Sir Robert escorted them to the sitting room on the ground floor. 'You must be happy with the outcome, Grace?'

'Thank you. I think it's gone rather well.'

'And you, *Woodpecker*? Will you return to East Berlin?'

'Not now. Ludmilla will be informed of my death, and she will receive a senior KGB officer's pension. So, I'll stay in Paris for a few days. Until things calm down a bit. I may come back to London briefly, then I'll take a long, one way holiday somewhere.'

'Anywhere in mind?' Grace asked.

'Possibly Hong Kong.' Ivkin sat heavily in the green leather chair. 'And Alistair?'

'What about him?' Grace asked.

'Should he be told?'

'No. As far as he is concerned, you are dead. And, it should stay that way. But here is something interesting for you to contemplate. The passport in the name of John Pevington was given by Sir Giles Merrick-Smith to Alistair. So, as far as Sir Giles is concerned, if John Pevington is dead, Alistair Quinn is dead.'

There was silence for a few minutes before Sir Richard spoke. 'Oh Grace, if I didn't know differently, I would have thought you'd put Sir Giles up to it.'

'Alistair has no attachments. He is completely selfish. For him, attachment is a tool of exploitation on the path of manipulation to total control.'

'Like mother, like son, perhaps? And the cultivation of trust?' Ivkin remarked.

Grace laughed. 'Trust! I think it highly unlikely that Alistair is capable of trust. But, perhaps for what I have in mind, he doesn't need it. He can travel the world, sleep with whom he chooses, live behind enemy lines, make large amounts of money and all for Queen and country. As persona non grata, he can go anywhere. To do anything. And with Grigori Ivkin dead, Frank Quinn can resurface.'

'But will you, Frank? Will you come back from the dead?' Sir Robert asked.

'Of course he will,' Grace replied. 'We always need people to remove traitors. Quietly. Unobserved. As far as the world is concerned Alistair Quinn, just like Frank Quinn, is dead. At least until he has a new identity.'

'Will you stop working for the Service, Frank?' Greaves asked.

'We never resign, Dickie. You know that. Besides, what would I do with myself? When you've lived on the edge of life, gardening just doesn't have the same appeal.'

'Safer!'

'Perhaps, but boring.'

'Definitely like father, like son.'

'Wouldn't Alistair just love that!' Grace said.

***

Alistair stood by the compacted grave and sniffed the early morning air. Pale light tinged the sky. The rain had abated during the time he was busy burying the Soviet driver. But he was wet through, from rain and sweat. He glanced at his coat which he'd secreted under a stone plinth and was the only item of his clothing that wasn't wet through. But he had more work to do before he could pull on his damp coat. The dead Soviet driver, Sergei was enormous, all muscle and sinew, and in death, he weighed almost more than Alistair could carry. In fact, he'd had to drag the corpse out of the car and across the gravel. He then rolled the awkwardly stiffened man into the hole that had taken him over two hours to dig. Alistair had stood staring at the corpse. He was another man who worked in the shadows now consigned to the earth, nameless, forgotten to all but those who'd killed him. He wondered if Irina would forget she'd killed the unsuspecting man. She'd shown no remorse, no fear, nor any lack of courage. Sergei whatever-his-name-was, had no mourners, no family to weep, no headstone to testify he'd ever lived. Alistair then had walked back to where Julian Murray lay dead on the ground and grasping him under his shoulders, had manhandled him into the car. Murray was not as heavy as the driver, but his lifeless body was awkward to manoeuvre. Sitting him on the seat, Alistair had swung his legs into the car then leaned the body forward over the steering wheel making sure the Makarov pistol was on the seat beside him. Then using his feet, he'd covered the drag marks in the gravel and dirt. When this was done, he took the shovel and pick and walked some distance from the grave to leave it lying under some shrubs about four hundred yards away. By the time he returned to the gravesite, he was hungry, thirty and exhausted. He checked the site once more then pulled on his near-dry coat. He was about to leave when he heard the crunch of footsteps on the gravel path and looked up.

Through the trees, he saw a little distance away a lone figure walking along the drive into the cemetery. Alistair hid behind a nearby headstone and watched. The man approached the Soviet car where the bloodied dead body of Julian Murray lay slumped over the steering wheel, the passport of John Pevington in his shirt pocket. The man carried a weapon. A machine gun in his right hand. Alistair watched. The man didn't touch the car nor inspect it. Surely an early morning mourner would be surprised to see a car there at that hour. Unless, of course, he already knew what or who was inside. Alistair held his breath. Waiting only a few minutes, he saw the man walk directly to the grave of the Soviet driver.

Alistair hung back and watched.

Using his heel, the man removed some of the soil. Alistair stared, his eyes fixed on the man's activities. Then he placed a rifle into the hole. Again using his feet, he recovered the grave and stamped it down. Alistair watched as this man then threw a handful of gravel over the soil, finally taking a brass urn filled with pink flowers from another grave and placing it on the mound. He then stood and waited by the grave. But from what Alistair could tell, he was not a mourner.

At exactly 04.00 another man arrived. This man Alistair recognised as the passenger in the Soviet bulletproof car that had attempted to assassinate Friedleman in Place St Michel and the same car he'd seen stopped on the bridge. In the pre-dawn stillness he heard the cars. Several crunched their way along the drive. It resembled a cortège of mourners attending an early morning burial. But the cars drove on, parking further into the cemetery. Moments later, a siren blared, the car driving at speed towards the two men. It stopped in front of them. A flock of early morning sparrows instantly lifted off the surrounding trees into the air and vanished. Alistair squatted behind the headstone, his eyes fixed on the car which now blocked the main drive leading to the grave where the two men stood. Suddenly, both men were surrounded by gendarmes. One was objecting loudly. Alistair heard his protestations. But the gendarmes were not listening. They led both men towards the waiting cars. Then the unexpected happened.

What he saw left him speechless. One man had attempted to escape. A gendarme fired his pistol. The man fell. Then two more shots. The bigger man was still loudly protesting. He was bundled into a car. Alistair heard the engine start, and it drove away. His gaze went to the fallen man, still lying in the long grass. Alistair felt his pulse stop.

One car remained. He heard the car door open, and his mother got out. Alistair watched her walk towards the dead man who lay on the grass. He heard her call out, 'He's gone'. A second later, the dead man sat up. Alistair felt his heart skip a beat. His mouth fell open. So spellbound was he that he couldn't think. He felt faint at what he was witnessing. He stayed crouching behind a tombstone.

The car drove away. Alistair was alone now in the graveyard. What he'd witnessed left him feeling devoid of life. He felt nothing, empty, no emotion, no fear, no fright. His father, Frank Quinn was alive and had just performed another staged death. Alistair felt the anger rising. Within seconds, it was rage and profound betrayal. Neither his father nor his mother had thought it necessary to include or inform him that his father had not died that night in London. In fact, the truth of his father's death had been deliberately withheld from him. A staged death then and another now. How many times had this scenario been played out? For Frank Quinn life went on. Living. Dying. Living again. Until one day he wouldn't get up. Or no bulletproof vest would save him. And all played out on either side of the Berlin Wall. But Frank Quinn was a man without an identity, a name only and one who only existed in shadows and who belonged with the dead. In his head, Alistair heard his mother's voice. *Go home Simon Cordery*, she'd said. Nameless. No true identity. Only the one MI5 gave you and even that was temporary. Go home. Home. Where was that? It didn't exist with his parents. It was a safe house in Knightsbridge. A room with a silk robe and velvet slippers and free whisky to deaden reality. And who was Simon Cordery? Another fake identity. One of just thousands he'd have over time. If he stayed. If he played their game. His thoughts lingered on his father. He'd thought he'd glimpsed the real Frank Quinn in Finland and on the voyage back to Britain in '65. But that Frank Quinn only existed in fiction. Or only when Frank Quinn allowed anyone, even his son, into his secret world. Born in the Special Operations Executive of the Second World War, Frank Quinn had become addicted to high stakes espionage. And Grace Quinn, his mother, had aided it, and together they'd formed the identity of a single entity; a code, an enigma named *Woodpecker.*

Alistair walked to the corner and waited in the morning light until a cab drove by, numb by what he'd witnessed. Hailing it, he jumped in. 'International Airport,' he said to the driver. He rummaged in his pockets for the two passports he had with him. One in his real name and the other for Simon Cordery. He decided to use Simon Cordery's passport. When he didn't arrive at the British Embassy in Paris, nor in the flat in Rue de la Huchette or anywhere in Paris, or in London, his mother would put a search out for him and find where Simon Cordery had disappeared. But wherever the first long haul flight out of Paris took him, Simon Cordery would also disappear. Then Alistair Quinn would change aeroplanes or take a train or a bus or hitch-hike to somewhere else. Then he'd find another corrupt barman from whom he'd buy a fake passport. And disappear again to somewhere. He didn't care where.

Acknowledgements

I wish to thank my friend Ailsa Eckel for her enthusiastic diligence with copy editing. Also, to Günter Koch for advising me on life in East Berlin in the 1960s. My thanks also to my friend Linda Huchinson who accompanied me to Paris and walked miles with me in that lovely city, ensuring the accuracy of the locations. My thanks also go to Brittany Wilson who designed the cover, to AnneMarie Brear for her wonderful help and kindness and to my friend AWBL for the inspiration to write this series. And finally, as ever, I wish to thank my dear late husband and greatest supporter, Peter, who heard the early chapters of this story before leukaemia took him.

About the author

After leaving school, Victoria trained as a primary teacher then as a nurse, specialising in burns care. While working in the health industry, she studied singing at the NSW Conservatorium and went on to work in a semi-professional capacity for over twenty years.

Coming into writing later in life has meant that her varied life experiences, coupled with a love of history, have had a strong influence on her writing. She is a #1 Best Seller on Amazon, a Publisher's Weekly Star Reviewed Author, a Gold Medal winner, a twice Silver Medal winner and Bronze Medal winner in the Global Book Awards for 2023, 2024 and 2025. She has been interviewed by the BBC in England and on London Radio and also by Dan Snow's *History Hit*. In 2025, the Clement Wisdom series was selected to be included in the Australian War Memorial.

She is married with two children and four grandchildren and lives in the Southern Highlands of New South Wales.

Visit her website at www.vmknoxauthor.com

Also by

Neither Despise Nor Fear Series

Neither Despise Nor Fear

1965 and Alistair Quinn is sixteen. Making a sudden and life-changing decision, he runs away from his prestigious North London school and heads straight for the bright lights of Soho. In a brothel there he meets a prominent politician and a Soviet KGB officer; one both MI6 and the CIA hope to turn double agent. Recruited into MI5, he becomes embroiled in a high stakes mission of deception, treachery and death where no one is who they seem.

The Clement Wisdom Series

In Spite of All Terror

In Spite of All Terror is the first in a series of WWII crime / espionage thrillers. Set in September 1940, when Britain stood alone against an imminent Nazi invasion, Reverend Clement

Wisdom and other men from the restricted occupations, join the covert Auxiliary Units. Based in East Sussex, these ordinary men by day must become saboteurs and assassins by night. Following the murders of several of Clement's team, he becomes embroiled in the murky world of espionage when things are never what they seem.

If Necessary Alone

If Necessary Alone is the second thriller in the World War II series. Clement Wisdom, now a Major in Special Duties Branch of the Secret Intelligence Service (MI6) is sent to remote Caithness in Northern Scotland to investigate illicit encrypted radio transmissions. As soon as he arrives there, an out-station wireless operator is found brutally murdered, and Clement becomes entangled in a web of death and silence. Alone, and in the bitter Scottish winter, Clement must stay one step ahead of a killer if he is to remain alive.

Where Death and Danger Go

Where Death and Danger Go is set in the dark days of 1941. Britain fights on alone. Invasion and fear hang in the air. On a winter's night, a German spy parachutes into Cambridgeshire as another man is murdered nearby. Is he another enemy spy or has he been sent to his death? Either way, a killer lurks. Major Clement Wisdom of the SIS is sent to investigate and discovers a web of conspiracy where kidnap, murder and revenge threaten his life and the safety of the nation.

West Wind Clear

By late 1941, the Pacific is a very different place, and Japan threatens the security of the region. As Clement is preparing to return to Britain from Australia, he is seconded to lead a small guerrilla force to Singapore, where he is to rescue an import man who is carrying a vital secret. After the apparent suicide of one of his team, Clement becomes suspicious that an enemy spy is among them; one who will kill to safeguard his identity.

Code Name Sorrow

Major Clement Wisdom of the SIS is in Sydney, Australia to learn Morse Code and its Japanese equivalent Kana Morse. But when a fellow student from the college is found dead and another missing, Clement begins to suspect espionage. While assisting the local police, Clement uncovers a network of enemy spies, fuelled by long held resentments and treacherous greed. In May 1942, three Japanese submarines entered Sydney Harbour. Their intention was to destroy the *USS Chicago* and as many other Allied ships berthed there. Or was there another reason?

Printed in Dunstable, United Kingdom

79213282R00194